Who Ghost There?

THE GHOST DETECTIVE MYSTERIES - BOOK 6

JANE HINCHEY

· BAYWOLF PRESS ·
BP
BAYWOLF PRESS

AUTHOR'S NOTE

Hey! Welcome to the weird and wacky world of my imagination. I hope you enjoy your time here.

If you love anything supernatural as much as I do, then you're going to enjoy the journey ahead - at least I think you will.

Give up the Ghost is the second book in my Ghost Detective series, with more to come, so make sure you sign up for my newsletter to get notifications on when the next book is ready.

You can sign up for my newsletter here:
Janehinchey.com/subscribe

Okay, ready to weave some magic and solve some mysteries?

I'll see you on the other side!

xoxo

Jane

FREE BOOK OFFER

Want to get an email alert when the next Ghost Detective Mystery is available? Sign up for my newsletter today, https://janehinchey.com/subscribe and as a bonus, receive a FREE e-book of **Cupcakes & Curses!**

About this Book

Running a private eye firm in Firefly Bay would be so much easier if I didn't have a dozen elderly ghosts dogging my every step.

All I really want is to solve my cases, enjoy my coffee in peace, date super-hot cop *Captain Cowboy Hot Pants*, or, as he likes to be called, Detective Kade Galloway, and keep my annoyingly loveable family from discovering my ghost whispering secret.

But before I can say *café au lait,* I have a dead nurse on my hands whose death was no accident, a house overrun with supernatural seniors, a talking cat who has zero appreciation that the diet I put him on is in his own best interests (his furball presents inside my shoes are totally uncalled for), and an intriguing new neighbor who has busted me (more than once) talking to ghosts.

Fingers crossed, I can solve the mystery of why I am suddenly a ghost magnet and convince the dearly departed to move on before I'm carted off in a straightjacket.

Chapter One

There are a dozen ghosts in my kitchen, and none of them are talking. They turned up three days ago—seven women, five men, all aged in their seventies or older, and despite my attempts to engage, not one of them has spoken a word. Nada. Zip. Zilch. This is unusual because normally, when a ghost finds me, they've unexpectedly departed the mortal realm and are a tad confused about what in the ever-living-heck is going on.

Not these guys. Nope, they're just hovering around my kitchen. If only they'd make themselves useful while they were here, but no, my dishes aren't done, nor is my coffee freshly made and waiting for me each morning. A bit of an ask considering they're incorporeal and can't touch anything, but the sentiment remains.

Padding across the floor, I shooed a gray-haired woman out of the way to reach the coffee machine. She obligingly moved.

"Are any of you Cecilia?" I asked, grabbing a cup from the overhead cupboard. Glancing over my shoulder, my eyes darted from one ghost to the next, checking for any signs of recognition. Nothing. Not even the tiniest of sparks. "Can you even hear me?" It was rhetorical. They hadn't responded since they arrived, yet they were aware of me; otherwise, they wouldn't move out of my way when I shooed them. Not that it was entirely necessary. I could just walk through them, but *ewww*. Plus, touching a ghost was a chilly business, and I did my best to avoid it.

"Morning, Audrey." Ben, my best friend and resident ghost who I could see, hear, and communicate with, appeared. "Visitors still here, I see." He slid onto a bar stool, watching me wait for my brew.

"Hey, Ben. How goes it?" Since Ben was a ghost and therefore didn't need sleep, he'd taken to visiting with insomniac neighbors, hanging out as they watched Netflix or, preferably, some late-night shopping channel while I slept. That's what Ben missed the most since his death... his secret addiction to shopping.

"Hey, I saw something you might like." He grinned, leaning forward to rest his elbow on the breakfast bar, only his elbow disappeared beneath the surface. "It was this yellow—"

"Nuh-uh!" I held my hand up in a stop gesture, cutting him off. "Too early. Need coffee."

"Did this lot keep you up?"

I shook my head. They weren't much of a bother, provided you didn't mind them following you around. While I'd slept, they'd spent the night hovering in my bedroom. Even my cat, Thor, and my raccoon, Bandit, had become accustomed to their presence.

"God, I hope they're not here to stay," I muttered to myself. The coffee machine had done its job, and I picked up my steaming brew, cupping it between my palms and lifting it, inhaling the decadent scent as the steam wafted up into my face. Closing my eyes, I took a sip, schooling my features as I burned my lips and tongue, hoping the rapid watering of my eyes didn't spill over and run down my cheeks.

"Hot?" Ben asked drolly. I ignored him. We'd done this many times before, and honestly, you'd think I'd learn by now to give my coffee a minute or two to cool down, but when it came to caffeine, all bets were off. As was common sense, apparently.

"Are you sure you can't communicate with them?" I cocked my head toward the senior citizens, now standing motionless behind Ben.

"I've tried. I can try again, I guess." He rubbed his chin and eyeballed the ghosts.

"And you don't recognize any of them from the home?" Ben's dad, Bill Delaney, was currently residing in Firefly Bay's Aged Care Facility, suffering from Alzheimer's. When the ghosts had first appeared, I'd panicked and thought something had happened to

Bill, but Ben had checked, and his father was fine.

Ben shook his head. "Nope. All I can tell you is that their most recent death is Cecilia Fairweather, seventy-two. Died in her sleep last week."

I scratched my head. "None of this makes sense."

"Mom, Mom, Mom!" Bandit burst through the cat door, skidding across the floor as she attempted to evade the ghosts. Thor, my overweight British shorthair cat, followed, his belly barely making it through the cat door, his back legs wiggling in the air as he eventually squeezed through. Under the vet's instructions, Thor was now on a diet and none too happy about it.

"What is it, Bandit?" The raccoon was on her hind legs, front paws scratching at my thigh, leaving welts beneath my pajama pants. I scratched behind her ears, then gently removed her from my leg before she drew blood.

"We have new neighbors!"

"Someone is moving in next door," Thor added, his British accent adorable. "Maybe they have treats?" He about-faced, heading back toward the cat door.

"Thor!"

He stopped, and his orange eyes shot me a look of utter disdain.

"Do not go over there begging for food," I said, pointing a finger at him.

If cats could raise their eyebrows, that is what I imagined him to be doing, for his whiskers moved, and then his eyes narrowed and his tail flicked. I could practically see the cogs turning.

I turned to Ben. "You talk to him." I sighed. "Maybe he'll listen to you." Thor had been Ben's cat before Ben had been murdered. And ever since that fateful day, I'd not only been able to see ghosts, but it turned out I could talk to animals too. Well, Thor and Bandit, at any rate.

"Thor, buddy, come on," Ben obliged. "You know Audrey only wants to keep you healthy. The vet says it's not good for you to carry too much weight."

"It's called emotional eating." Thor sniffed. "I'm distressed that you're dead."

Oh, Thor was good. Ben crumbled like a house of cards. He bent down and attempted to fuss over his cat, but of course, couldn't. He was incorporeal. He couldn't physically touch anything. I looked on, wondering if there was a sliver of truth in Thor's words or if he was just manipulating us to get what he wanted. Food. Ben had been dead for over a year now, and while Thor had always been fond of food, the weight gain had been more recent, leading me to believe it wasn't grief-related but glutton-related.

The theme song to *Ghostbusters* rang out, startling me, and I glared at my phone before picking it up. "Did you change the ringtone again?"

Ben grinned, straightening. "Maybe." It was the one thing he could do as a ghost. Manipulate the metadata of electronic devices. It came in handy on PI cases where he could access suspects' phones and tell me who they'd called or texted.

A quick glance at the screen told me it was my super-hot boyfriend and Firefly Bay Police Department's best ever detective,

Captain Cowboy Hot Pants, aka Kade Galloway.

"Hey, babe, what's up?" I answered.

"Has a new ghost turned up at your place?" he asked furtively.

I did a quick headcount. "No. I have my usual dozen, plus Ben. Why's that?"

Galloway sighed. "There's been an accident."

"You suspect foul play?" I didn't need to ask if someone had died. Clearly, there'd been a death, or he wouldn't have asked about a new ghost. "Is the victim elderly?"

"No. She's twenty-one."

"Oh, how awful. That's young. But sorry, she hasn't turned up here."

"Could you meet me at the scene? See if she's, you know, hanging around?"

"Sure. Just let me get dressed, and I'll be there in a few." I jotted down the address and had just hung up when the twelve silent ghosts suddenly found their vocal cords. They all looked at me and said in unison, "Angel."

I couldn't contain the scream that involuntarily slipped out, along with a little pee. Lord almighty, but I hadn't been expecting that!

"Angel?" I repeated, hand to my heart, trying to soothe the frantic beating from the fright they'd just given me.

"Angel," they said again. Then again. And again. I clapped my hands over my ears and raced upstairs, cursing my ghost-hearing abilities. They'd better not keep this up. Silent hovering ghosts I could handle, but not if they were going to chant *angel* every minute.

I got dressed in record time, jeans and T-shirt, and had just shoved my foot into my canvas sneaker when something cold and wet and utterly gross squelched between my toes. Trying not to gag and failing, I pulled my foot out, cat vomit dripping from my toes.

"Thor!" I bellowed. Of course, the furry critter wasn't going to respond. No doubt he'd gone next door to ingratiate himself with our new neighbors. I made a mental note to drop in myself and say hi and ask them ever so politely not to fall for his tricks. After rinsing my foot off in the bath, I found a clean pair of shoes, checked for cat barf, then hurried downstairs, wondering if lap band surgery was a thing for felines.

Chapter Two

The accident scene was hard to miss, given the flashing lights of two police cars and an ambulance. We were a few miles out of town, a quiet road usually. I pulled over, killed the engine, and hopped out of my Honda CR-V. Galloway stood on the other side of the road and raised his hand in greeting. Checking for oncoming traffic first, I hurried across.

"The victim's name isn't Angel by any chance?" I asked, accepting the kiss he dropped on my cheek.

"No. Why?" Galloway took my hand and led me to where a green Chevrolet Spark sat with the front end crumpled against a tree trunk. *Ouch.*

I dropped my voice. "You know my twelve guests? Just after your call, they all started saying the name Angel."

"What do you think it means?"

"Well, I thought maybe it was your victim's name, but I have to say, it's creepy, the way they all say it in unison without any emotion or inflection. Straight out of a horror movie." I shuddered, remembering.

"Are they here yet?" Galloway glanced around as if he could see them for himself, bless his cotton socks.

"Not yet. But they'll be here soon." I'd discovered the ghosts could track me down wherever I was, but they didn't appear and disappear like Ben did. They traveled in a pack, slowly, and I'd often see them coming, giving me time to escape. Or at least temporarily delay the inevitable.

I looked at the crumpled car. "Lost control and hit the tree?" I guessed, glancing from the front end of the Spark to the curve in the road behind us.

Galloway nodded. "Looks that way. Happened sometime during the night. A passing motorist saw the car this morning and stopped. So," he dropped his voice and bent so he was speaking directly into my ear, "can you see her?"

"A young woman, you said?"

"Yeah. Molly Lewis. Twenty-one. Shoulder-length, curly brown hair, brown eyes. Wearing blue jeans and a bright floral top."

I nodded, then perused the scene. All I could see were cops and ambulance personnel. This stretch of road was isolated, with no onlookers hovering to catch a glimpse.

"Sorry." I shook my head. "She's not here. She's moved on."

Galloway rubbed at the back of his neck. "I thought for sure she'd be one of your... visitors."

"Why's that? This was an accident, wasn't it?" I eyeballed the crushed car. The driver's side door was open, the airbags had deployed and subsequently deflated. She must have been traveling at a decent speed for them not to have saved her. I leaned in closer and peered at the windscreen. Shattered from the impact but intact. There was no indication that she'd hit it with her head, so I assumed she was wearing her seatbelt.

"It looks like an accident," Galloway agreed, rocking back on his heels. "Driving too fast, came to a bend, lost control. But there's something that puzzles me."

"Oh?"

"See here?" He pointed to the ground.

"What am I looking at?" I asked, not seeing anything other than dirt.

"Drag marks. Hidden. Scuffed over. But it looks like Molly was dragged from the passenger side of the car to the driver's side."

I frowned. "You sure? I don't see anything." Yes, the ground was scuffed, but then a dozen emergency personnel had been all over the site. It wasn't surprising there were marks in the dirt.

"Molly wasn't behind the wheel," Galloway added. I paused in my fruitless examination of the ground and looked at him, waiting for him to elaborate. "She was lying on the ground by the driver's door."

"So, she was conscious after she hit the tree? Probably tried to get out, to get help." It would be an instinctive reaction, wouldn't it? If you crashed your car, especially head-on, there was probably smoke coming from beneath the hood. My instinct would be to get my butt out of the vehicle in case the whole thing went up in flames. Despite Galloway telling me a million times that rarely happens and what we see in the movies isn't real, I suspect if it had been me behind the wheel, I'd have crawled away to a safe distance and then tried to call for help. "Where's her phone?"

"In her purse."

"And it was still in the car?"

"Yes. Passenger footwell. If we assume she was driving, then it was probably on the passenger seat and fell to the floor in the crash."

I was nodding in agreement when I heard it. Not the sound of twelve approaching ghosts chanting Angel, but music. Faint. I cocked my head, straining to hear. What was that? "*Black Magic*," I said under my breath.

"What's that?" Galloway asked.

"Can you hear music?" I glanced around, then peered inside Molly's car. Was the radio on?

"No."

"I hear that song from a girl group. *Black Magic*." I sang a few lines.

"Little Mix?"

My eyes narrowed. "You listen to Little Mix?"

"Hey," he laughed, giving me a playful nudge with his elbow, "I'm a well-rounded guy. It isn't all death metal and country, you know."

"It's not even death metal."

A tow truck arrived, reverse alarm blaring as it backed up and prepared to hoist Molly's car onto its tray.

"Well," I reached up on tip-toe and kissed Galloway lightly on the lips, "this one is all yours. I've got to get home. Thor puked in my shoe—again—and I have new neighbors moving in that I need to warn not to give in to any begging shenanigans and feed him." Since it looked like Molly's death had been an accident, and there was no ghost for me to ask, there was nothing for me to do here.

"New neighbors? Who?"

"No idea, but I shall find out. I'll see you later."

After jogging back to my car, I climbed in, executed a sixty-seven-point U-turn, and was heading back toward town when I came across my twelve ghosts. It was impossible to avoid them, spread across the road as they were. They gave me no choice but to drive right through. I probably shouldn't have closed my eyes because when I blinked them open, I'd nearly run off the road. Quickly correcting, I caught a glimpse of the ghosts in the rearview as they re-grouped, about-faced, and followed.

"Was that what happened to Molly?" I wondered out loud. "Fell asleep at the wheel?" All it takes is one minute of inattentiveness, and boom, hello tree. The radio was on; Pink's latest release had just finished playing when *Black Magic* by Little Mix came on. I scowled at the radio. This couldn't be a coincidence, could it? I swore I heard that song playing at the accident scene. And now it was playing on the radio.

"Molly?" I asked, eyes darting around the interior of my car, checking the rearview, trying to catch a glimpse of an errant ghost. Nothing. She wasn't here. Odd. It was all very odd.

To say my new neighbor was an Adonis was an understatement. I stood on his front porch, a paper bag containing a muffin from Nick's Bodega clutched in my hand, and simply stared. I'm pretty sure my mouth was hanging open, and there was a high probability of drool. I blinked and absently wiped my chin.

"Hey," the Adonis repeated, "you okay? Can I get you something? Water?"

I shook myself out of my stupor and thrust the paper bag at him. "Audrey. Next door," I eloquently introduced myself. He smiled, ignoring the paper bag, and I practically swooned.

"Sebastian Castle. Call me Seb. Come on in." He stood back and waved me inside. "Excuse all the boxes."

Seb was tall, and I mean tall, well over six foot, with dirty blond hair cut short but styled in luxurious waves on top, electric blue eyes, and one hundred percent smoking hot. If I weren't dating Galloway, I'd seriously consider throwing my hat in the ring with Seb. But Galloway had my heart, which meant Seb was simply eye candy, and I could live with that.

"Er. I just wanted to say hi and welcome you to the neighborhood," I said, still holding the muffin bag because he hadn't taken it from me. Now I didn't know what to do with it and felt like an idiot. I hadn't been prepared for just how attractive he was. He'd taken the air clean out of my sails, but I was regrouping, and I plastered a smile on my face. "And also, if my cat—or raccoon—comes over here begging for food, please don't feed them. They are not starving as they like to make out. They are, in fact, very well fed. Too well fed. Thor is on a diet."

"And is Thor the cat or raccoon?" One perfectly sculpted brow rose.

"Thor is the cat. He's a gray British shorthair. Totally adorbs, but you know," I made a motion with my hand over my belly, "round."

Seb chuckled. "Gotcha. No feeding Thor and the raccoon. Are they likely to come over here?"

I snorted. "For food? Most definitely. The raccoon is Bandit. Just in case, you know, you wanted to know."

Seb grinned. "No problem. I look forward to meeting them. Audrey, wasn't it?"

"Audrey Fitzgerald." I nodded. Placing the muffin bag on top of a box, I held out my hand. Seb shook it. He had a nice handshake. Not too firm, not too limp. Just... nice.

"Nice to meet you, Audrey Fitzgerald." He smiled, white teeth dazzling in his tanned face. "So, no work today?"

I frowned. "What?"

"Well, it's Friday. And you're home. So... day off? Or are you a stay-at-home mom?"

I balked at that. "I'm a private investigator," I shot back. "I work from home."

He blinked. "Wow! A PI? That is amazing. And fascinating."

"And you?" I dutifully asked. Male model. He had to be a male model or movie star. There was nothing else for it given that bone structure, symmetry, and just the overall package, really.

"I'm a teacher."

Get out! I cleared my throat, cocked my head, and asked, "Sorry? Did you say… *teacher?*"

He laughed. "I get that a lot. Yes. I'm an elementary school teacher. I teach third grade."

"I bet the moms love you," I muttered under my breath.

Seb cupped a hand around his ear. "Sorry? What was that? I didn't catch it."

"I said I bet the kids love you," I lied, smiling and showing all my teeth. "Well." I shifted from one foot to the other, glanced around at the mountain of boxes, and swung my arms. "I'll leave you to it. Umm, welcome again, and please, let me know if Thor and Bandit are a nuisance."

"I promise not to feed them." He saluted. "Well, nothing but healthy snacks," he added. Oh, boy. Thor and Bandit were going to love him.

Chapter Three

I was standing on the back lawn, hosing out
my puke-filled shoe, surrounded by my
twelve now thankfully silent ghosts and Ben
when it happened. With the hose in hand, I
was chatting with Ben, bemoaning the fact
that Thor's retaliation of the diet regimen
he's currently on—recommended by the vet
if you don't mind—has resulted in an all-out
war between me and my—his—beloved cat
when Seb's voice came from right
behind me.

"Who are you talking to?" he asked.

I let out a short, startled scream and turned, squirting him in the chest with the hose. So, there we stood, both of us looking stunned, only he was now a contestant in a wet T-shirt competition.

"Do you think you could, you know, turn that off?" he asked, water continuing to pour down his front.

"Right! Sorry!" I crimped the hose, halting the flow. "I was talking to myself," I added, then pointed to my drenched shoe. "Thor is on a diet, and he's taken to letting me know his displeasure by vomiting in my footwear."

"Right." Seb attempted to wring the moisture from his T-shirt.

"Sorry about that." I nodded to his shirt. "You startled me."

His face split into a wide smile. "Yeah, I got that. Only…it was as if you were listening to someone answering you."

My own smile slipped. It was getting harder to keep my ghost-talking abilities under wraps. My family was becoming more and more suspicious. The last thing I needed was my sister-in-law Amanda on my case about talking to spirits. She'd have me booked into a psych facility before I could blink. As it was, we were at an uneasy truce about her trying to fix my clumsiness. No need to rock that particular boat.

"Who would I have been talking to?" I waved around the empty garden. "There's no one here." No one except the thirteen ghosts and us.

He lowered his head, a sheepish expression darting across his face. "You're right! I don't know. Call it the stress of moving."

"Where do you hail from, Seb?" I asked, crossing to the tap and turning off the hose.

"My term was up in the city, so I applied for a position at Firefly Bay Elementary School, and here I am."

"So, you're renting?"

"Oh, no, I bought this place. I'm looking to put down roots. It's time for this bachelor to settle down."

"Ooooooh, boy," Ben muttered, "this one is going to be dangerous."

"What do you mean?" I asked, shooting Ben a look.

Seb looked at me as if I had two heads. "What do I mean? I'm... I thought that was pretty apparent. But I'm looking to make a home. Settle down. Have kids." He scratched his head and smiled.

"Busted," Ben snickered, but I didn't fall for it again. This time, I kept my eyes firmly glued on Seb.

"Right, sorry." I shook my head. "I'm really not focusing today. So, was there anything I could help you with? Not with the getting a wife part, but you came over here for a reason?" I gushed, feeling my cheeks heat.

"I was hoping I could bum a cup of coffee?" he asked hopefully. "Until I find the box I packed the coffee maker in, I have to buy take-out, and I really don't feel like heading into town just for a cup of coffee."

"Of course! Not a problem. Come on in." I waved toward the sliding glass doors on my back deck while I retrieved my wet shoe. Shaking out as much water as I could, I carried it to the deck, placing it to catch as much sun as possible. Who knows if the canvas would survive the cat puke and drenching I'd just given it, but I had to at least try.

Seb preceded me inside, stopped with hands-on-hips to look around the large open plan kitchen, dining, and living room. He whistled. "Nice place."

"Thanks." I shrugged, busying myself with the coffee maker. "It was my friend's. I inherited it."

"Oh, your friend died? I'm so sorry. That's tough."

"Yeah. Just over a year ago now. He left me this house, his PI business, and Thor."

"Oh, so the cat isn't yours?"

"He is now."

"So, this vomiting in your shoe thing? Do you think that's him acting out because he misses his owner?"

I was already shaking my head. "Nope. Oh, I know he misses him, but this is all diet-related. Is it possible for cats to have food disorders?"

"Maybe, I guess? Like, it could be an anxiety thing." Seb wandered into the living room, examining the books on the shelves, three of which were mine.

"I think I like him," Ben said, leaning against the counter next to me, crossing his arms over his chest he watched Seb peruse the titles.

"Me too," I whispered out of the corner of my mouth. "He's an upgrade on Mrs. Hill."

Ben turned his attention to me. "You don't *like* like him, do you? What about Galloway?"

I hit his chest in outrage. Or at least I tried to. My hand passed right through him. "How dare you," I hissed. "I am allowed to have male friends and not have them mean anything other than friendship. Hello!" I pointed from him to me and back again. "Case in point."

Ben nodded. "Gotcha. But I gotta say, Seb is a good-looking rooster."

"I'm not blind," I snapped, then glanced over at the good-looking rooster in question only to discover he was watching me, head cocked to one side.

"Okay, I confess," I raised my voice and grinned ruefully, "you're going to find this out about me eventually, so I may as well spill."

"What are you doing?" Ben snapped, standing bolt upright.

"Oh? What's that?" Seb asked, curiosity piqued.

I held up my hand and counted off on my fingers. "The first thing is that I'm clumsy. Incredibly clumsy. I'm kinda famous for it in Firefly Bay. Especially if you talk to my family." I held up a second finger. "And I talk to myself. A lot. Animated conversations, like you just witnessed."

"Ahhhh. That explains it." Seb grinned, then turned his attention back to the bookshelf. "You're into thrillers, I see."

"Those are Ben's." I finished preparing the coffee and placed his on the kitchen bench. "Here you go."

He crossed the room in long easy strides. "Audrey Fitzgerald, you're a lifesaver." He picked up the coffee cup, clinked it with mine, and took a sip, making an exaggerated sighing sound. "Nirvana," he breathed, eyes closed. "I can see us being great friends," Seb continued, opening his dazzling blue eyes and pinning me to the spot.

"Wait until you meet my boyfriend." I grinned. "You're going to love him."

"Nice segue, Fitz." Ben nodded in approval. I continued to ignore him. It wasn't easy.

"He's a detective for the Firefly Bay Police Department," I continued. "Detective Kade Galloway."

"That's awesome!" Seb smiled, his impossibly white teeth flashing again. "Bring him over to say hi next time he's here. I'd love to meet him. Maybe he could come into the school and talk with the kids. I bet they'd love to meet a real-life detective." Seb held up his coffee cup. "Do you mind if I take this with me? I don't want to hold you up, and I've got a ton of unpacking to get to, not to mention change my shirt—I'll return the cup, of course."

"Oh, sure." I forced a smile, not caring one way or the other.

"He's running because he thinks you're a psycho." Ben smirked, arms crossed over his chest, watching Seb leave.

I frowned. "Do you really think he thinks that?"

"Hello? He's caught you twice in quick succession talking to thin air. Not to mention you squirted him with the hose. As soon as that coffee was in his hands, he was out of here."

"Oh, well." I took a sip of my own coffee. "Maybe it's for the best. Goodness knows it was hard enough to keep my secret when Mrs. Hill was living next door. I've gotten used to keeping my guard down in my own home."

The doorbell rang, jolting me out of my thoughts. Of course, whenever the doorbell rang, Thor and Bandit suddenly took on the persona of a dog. The pair of them came barreling down the stairs, skidding to a halt at the front door, the soft *thunk* echoing down the hallway as Bandit slid into the wall as she always did.

"Mom, Mom, Mom!" Bandit chanted. "Someone's here, someone's here." Like I hadn't heard the doorbell nor knew what it meant. Bless her.

While Thor was a little more subdued. "Don't worry, I'll get it," he said, although I always wondered how he intended to *get it* considering he couldn't actually get it. Smiling at the rambunctious pair, I stepped around them and opened the door.

"Are you the private investigator?" a woman in her early fifties demanded. She was a little bit plump, a little bit disheveled, and a whole lot angry.

"Yes. I'm Audrey Fitzgerald of Delaney Investigations," I said.

"Good. I need to hire you." She pushed past me, giving me no choice but to step aside before she trampled over the top of me.

"Come in," I said drolly. She stormed through the length of the house to the living area at the rear. I followed.

"Coffee?" I asked.

"Tea?"

I inclined my head. "Sure. Take a seat." I pointed to one of the stools at the breakfast bar, and while she seated herself, I grabbed the kettle and filled it with water. "Why don't you tell me what brought you here today?" I invited.

"My daughter…" She trailed off, and I glanced up from my tea-making preparations to see her chin wobble and a tear roll down her cheek. "My daughter died last night," she choked out. "And the police are saying it was an accident. That she was drunk driving."

I froze. Was her daughter Molly Lewis? The young woman Galloway had called me about earlier?

"I'm so sorry to hear that, Mrs…?"

"Lewis. Joan Lewis." She sniffed, and I crossed over to the coffee table to retrieve a box of tissues. Bringing them back, I placed them next to her.

"You don't think it was an accident?" I prompted.

"Molly was bright, clever, so funny," Joan said. "And smart. She would never drink and drive. Never."

Galloway hadn't mentioned anything about Molly drinking, but then, it had been early in the investigation. They probably hadn't run any tests yet.

"Did they do a toxicology report on her?" I asked.

"Results aren't back yet." Joan snatched a tissue and blew her nose. "But the police officer said he could smell it on her."

"That doesn't mean she was over the limit," I pointed out.

Mrs. Lewis nodded. "That's exactly what I said. I don't think this was an accident. I think Molly was murdered, and I want to hire you to find who did it."

I blinked in shock. "What makes you think it was murder?"

"Someone was with her. Someone knows what happened." Joan Lewis was clearly convinced of it. I cast my mind back to the accident scene. Galloway thought Molly had been moved. He'd thought maybe she'd been a passenger, and someone had dragged her around to the driver's side of the car.

"Any idea who?"

"Probably her boyfriend. Nick Davidson." Her nose screwed up, and her lips turned down. I got the impression Joan Lewis disapproved of her daughter's choice in boyfriends.

"What makes you say that?"

"She told me she was meeting up with him last night." Joan crumpled the tissue, clenching it in her fist. "So? Are you taking the job or not?"

"Of course, I'll help you find out what happened to your daughter, Mrs. Lewis. Let me run through my fee structure, and you can decide if you want to proceed."

Chapter Four

After seeing Joan out, I tucked the check she'd written into my purse and hurried upstairs to get changed. I'd been a little embarrassed to be having a business meeting in bare feet, ripped jeans, and a slightly damp T-shirt, and now that I had suspects to interview, a change of wardrobe was in order.

"Thor." I pointed to the furry gray lump on my bed. "No more puking in my shoes, okay?"

"It wasn't me," he blatantly lied.

"It wasn't me!" Bandit declared. Bandit was one hundred and ten percent utterly devoted to Thor. If he asked her to take the fall for him, she would. In the meantime, she mimicked pretty much everything he did. Did that include hacking up a furball on demand?

I held up two fingers to my eyes, then spun my hand to point to the two of them. "It goes for both of you. You gotta puke? Take it outside."

"Maybe there's not always time to take it outside." Thor sniffed.

"If it's such an issue, then I think you may need medical attention," I said, swiping through the hangers in the walk-in-closet. "Maybe a trip to the vet?"

There was a moment's silence, then Thor said, "Fine!" and I bit back a laugh.

I shimmied into a black pair of non-torn Levi's, a clean T-shirt, and grabbed my pink denim jacket before sliding my feet into matching pink Chucks, cursing myself for not thinking to check for cat vomit first. I caught a lucky break. They were puke-free. I rested each foot on the vanity in the bathroom to tie the laces, then finger-combed my hair, swiped my lashes with mascara, and ran some gloss over my lips. Once upon a time, when I worked as a temp, I'd apply a full face of make-up every day and spend what felt like hours trying to tame my wavy hair. Working for yourself had its perks, and enjoying a more casual appearance was one of them.

"I'm heading out. You two stay here, please, don't go bothering the new neighbor. I've already warned him not to feed you."

Thor sat up and turned his back in stony silence. I gave him a pat despite his rejection and scratched Bandit behind the ears. "Be good," I told her.

"We will, Mom."

Joan Lewis had told me Nick was a university student and worked part-time at a fast-food restaurant, working most lunchtimes. Given it was almost lunchtime, I figured he'd be at work. And I was right. Waiting in line at the burger joint, I studied the young man. He was tall and skinny, all long limbs and sharp angles. His hair was pulled back into a ponytail. He had dark skin and eyes so dark they looked black. I wondered if Joan Lewis didn't like Nick Davidson because he was black.

"Hi." He greeted me with a plastic smile. "What can I get for you today?"

"Hey, Nick, I'm a private investigator. I need to ask you some questions."

He blinked a few times, not knowing what to say. "What for?" he eventually asked.

"It's about Molly."

His brow furrowed. "What about her?"

Oh, crap, he didn't know! No one had told him his girlfriend was dead.

"Can you take a break? We need to talk in private."

Nick looked around, not knowing what to do. His manager came bustling in from the kitchen in the back. "What's going on here? You got a complaint?" He drilled me with a hard look.

"No complaints," I said. "But I need a word with Nick. In private. It's important."

"He's not due for a break for another half hour."

"I repeat. It's important. In fact, you might want to get someone in to cover the rest of his shift."

"Why? What's happened," Nick asked. "Oh my God, it's Grandma, isn't it? She died." Tears welled in his eyes, and I reached across the counter to touch his hand.

"Your grandma is fine, Nick," I said softly. I turned my attention to the manager. "He's taking his break *now*."

The manager threw up his arms. "Go ahead." He sounded one hundred percent disgruntled, but he'd given in.

We took a corner booth. "You said this was about Molly. What about her?" Nick asked, sliding in opposite me.

"Nick, Molly died in a motor vehicle accident last night," I said softly.

"What?" he whispered, blinking rapidly.

"I'm so sorry." I reached across the table and touched his hand again, doing my best to convey my sympathy.

"What..." He swallowed. "What happened?"

"We're not one hundred percent sure, other than her car appeared to be traveling at speed and failed to take a corner, crashing into a tree."

We sat in silence while I gave time for Nick to digest the news. "I can't believe it," he whispered. "I just saw her yesterday."

"Her mom hired me to investigate what happened." I slid my business card across the table.

"Aren't the police investigating?"

I nodded. "They are. And I'm sure they'll come to talk with you. And they're probably going to ask you the same questions I am."

"What questions? This was an accident, wasn't it? You said a car accident."

"Molly's mom doesn't think it was. And preliminary investigations reveal Molly may have been moved after the accident. Meaning someone was with her."

"Who?"

"You tell me. Where were you last night, Nick?"

He blinked a couple of times as if shocked I'd asked him such a thing. "I was in the city. Visiting my grandma. She's not well."

"Which is why you thought I'd come to tell you she'd passed."

He hung his head. "Yeah."

"So, you weren't with Molly?"

He shook his head. "No. Last I saw her was here, yesterday." He looked around the fast-food restaurant. "She dropped in on her lunch break."

"You were working?"

"Yeah. I do most lunch shifts. Speaking of, I'd better get back to work. The place is filling up, and I'm really not supposed to be on my break."

My eyebrows shot up in surprise. He wanted to go back to work after hearing his girlfriend had died? I watched him, my suspicions rising. Maybe Joan was right to suspect him. "Go ahead." I waved at the counter. "But if you think of anything, hear anything, please, give me a call." I pulled a business card from my bag and placed it on the table between us.

He picked up the card and slid it into his pocket. "Will do." He'd taken several steps, then swiveled on his heel and came back. "Thank you," he said softly. "For telling me about Molly. I loved her. I'll miss her." His eyes were glassy again, and he wiped the back of his hand across them.

"I'm sorry for your loss." It was such a banal thing to say, but I meant it. I knew what it was like to lose someone you cared about, and I wouldn't wish it on anyone. From a distance, I heard the mournful chant of Angel signaling the approach of my resident ghosts. With any luck, I could stay one step ahead of them.

Hurrying back to my car, I sat behind the wheel for a moment, thinking about my next move. Nick had seemed genuinely surprised and then upset at the news of Molly's death, and just as I'd been crossing him off my suspect list, he'd made the decision to go back to work. That struck me as all kinds of odd. Molly's mom was pointing her finger at Nick, and while I didn't think he'd killed Molly, something was definitely up. Something I was determined to get to the bottom of.

The ghostly twelve appeared at the end of the block, slowly making their way down the sidewalk toward me. Time to hit the road. Next stop, the Firefly Bay Aged Care Facility... maybe Molly's coworkers knew who she was with last night.

"Hey, Mr. Delaney, how are you doing today?" Sitting across from Ben's dad, I took a sip of the tea one of the carers had brought over. I wasn't much of a tea drinker, but I could choke it down when the situation warranted it.

Bill suffered from dementia, a symptom of his Alzheimer's. His short-term memory was gone, and his long-term memory wasn't doing much better. More often than not, Bill thought he was sixteen years old.

"What's your name again?" he asked, peering at me, brow furrowed as his mind struggled to remember.

"Audrey. Audrey Fitzgerald. I'm a friend of your son's." Not that he remembered having a son. My heart hurt for Ben and his dad.

"Are you here to take me to the zoo?" he asked, hands shaking. He looked frail, his legs impossibly thin beneath the crocheted blanket covering them. I chewed on my lip, berating myself for not visiting more often. Ben laid a comforting hand on my shoulder. I ignored the jolt of icy air at his touch.

"Not today," I soothed, taking another sip of tea. "I'm here to visit you."

"I like the zoo." Mr. Delaney said, more to himself than to me.

"What's your favorite animal?"

"Oh, that would be the beetle. A girl I like has one."

"He's talking about a VW Beetle. The car Mom used to drive when he first met her," Ben explained. "He talks about her a lot."

"Nice to see you have a visitor today, Bill." A nurse approached, pushing a medication trolley.

Bill flinched, physically leaning away from the nurse who'd stopped by the side of his chair. "I haven't seen you here before," she said to me. "Are you a relative?" It was an innocuous enough question, I suppose, but it was the tone that had my hackles rising.

"I'm a friend of the family and trustee of Bill's affairs," I replied, studying her intently.

I pegged her to be in her late fifties, maybe sixties. She had that air about her, the one that said her love for her job was long since gone, and she was only here for the paycheck while she waited for retirement day to roll around. "And you are?"

"R.N. Sharon Mooney." Her smile didn't meet her eyes, and Bill was leaning so far away from her he was in danger of toppling out of his chair. Sharon turned her attention to him. "Come on now, Bill, time for your pills."

"Don't want them!" Bill shouted. His yell startled me, and I spilled my tea. Snatching up the napkin by my elbow, I blotted at the spill, frowning as a wet spot appeared on the knee of my jeans. At least it'd wash out.

"I know you don't, love." Sharon sighed. "But you need them to keep you well."

I shot a glance at Ben, who was watching the proceedings with his arms crossed over his chest. He saw me looking and explained, "This is common. It's a result of his confusion. As long as she remains calm and doesn't force him, he'll take his meds."

"Right," I muttered under my breath, pretending to fuss with my tea-stained jeans rather than openly watch Sharon cajole Bill into taking his meds. She succeeded within minutes, and I couldn't hide my surprise.

"I've been nursing for thirty-five years," Sharon said. "I know a thing or two about my patients."

"I can see that." I was forced to re-evaulate my opinion of her. Maybe she wasn't as uncaring as I'd initially thought. Tired, yes. But uncaring, no. I'd watched how gentle she was with Bill, how soothing, and despite his initial reaction to her, he'd quickly settled and done as she wanted.

"Actually," I stood up as Sharon started to wheel the trolley away, "I was wondering if I could have a word?"

"Oh? You have concerns about Bill?"

I shook my head. "No. I can see you're taking excellent care of him. It's about one of your nurses. Best discussed in private." I shot a look at Bill, but he wasn't paying us any attention. His gaze was on the window and the garden outside.

Sharon studied me, her face unreadable before she gave a curt nod. "Let me finish my rounds, and then we can talk. Meet me in my office in, say—" she glanced at her watch "—twenty minutes."

"Sure. Thanks." I sat back down, smiling at Bill. "So, Bill, last time I was here, you told me you wanted to be a mechanic. Is that still the case?"

Bill's face lit up. His eyes twinkled, and he beamed at me. "Yes, ma'am, I sure do. I love cars. My girlfriend, Beryl, drives a VW Beetle, and she lets me tinker on the engine to practice, you know?"

We filled the next twenty minutes discussing Beryl Sanderson, Ben's mom. It moved me how much he loved her, still, though it was equally sad that he didn't remember marrying her, having a child—Ben—and her dying of cancer a few short years ago.

Chapter Five

Sharon's office was dominated by one desk with two computers back to back, a chair on either side of the desk, obviously a shared office situation.

"Take a seat," she offered, seating herself on one side of the desk and nodding toward the second chair. I sat, scooting sideways so I could see her around the monitor.

"How can I help?" she asked.

"I was hoping to talk to you about Molly Lewis," I began. Sharon cut me off before I could get any further.

"Look, I don't have much time." She glanced at her watch, brow furrowed. "Molly didn't turn up for her shift this morning, so we're short-staffed. She'd better have a good excuse. That's all I can say. What, exactly, is this all about anyway?"

If she'd let me finish, I would have told her already! Grinding my teeth, I continued, "I'm sorry to have to tell you that Molly didn't turn up for her shift this morning because she died last night."

Sharon gasped, her hand going to her throat while her body flopped back in her chair. "She's dead?" she squeaked.

I nodded. "Sorry for your loss. Were you close?"

Sharon's mouth opened and closed, no sound coming out. She pinched the bridge of her nose and lowered her chin to her chest. I waited while she struggled to pull herself together.

"How?" she croaked, not raising her head.

"A car accident."

"Right." She nodded as if it made perfect sense. Which, of course, it didn't, which was why I was here. Sharon cottoned on to that fact pretty fast.

"You suspect foul play?" She lifted her head and shot me a shrewd look from bleary eyes.

"What makes you ask that?" I hedged.

She snorted. "I know you're a private investigator. You're asking me about Molly. Someone hired you. Someone suspects something."

I shook my head. "Not necessarily. I was hired by her mom to find out what happened. I'm just here doing my job."

"Isn't that what the police are for? To find out what happened?"

"And I'm sure they'll be here soon, asking the same questions. I'm just trying to trace Molly's last movements, who she saw last, that type of thing."

Sharon sat up straight and rolled her shoulders, then turned to her computer, slowly typing with two fingers, the keys clacking. "Let me bring up her roster."

"I thought you said she was scheduled for this morning."

A flush of pink colored her cheeks, and she cleared her throat. "Yes. That's right, I did. Sorry... the news... it's just rattled me a bit, is all."

I reached across the desk and patted her arm. "Of course. I'm sorry. I know it must be a terrible shock to you. Were you and Molly friends as well as colleagues?"

"Not really." Sharon kept pecking away at the keyboard. "Oh, don't get me wrong, we were *work friends*. But we didn't socialize outside of work. I leave that sort of thing to the younger crowd. You probably want to talk to Angela Brady. She and Molly were as thick as thieves, although, come to think of it, I think they may have had a falling out recently. I haven't seen them together in the break room of late."

"Angela works here?" I pulled out my phone to note her name.

Sharon nodded. "She's a nursing assistant, like Molly." She finally found what she was looking for on the computer and hit print. The behemoth printer behind her roared to life, spitting out a copy of Molly's schedule. Sharon snatched it from the printer and handed it to me. "Here you go. That's all I can tell you about her work movements. She was on days this week."

"Right. Well." I stood, paper clutched in my hand. "Thanks for your time. If you think of anything, anything at all, please give me a call." I placed a business card on the desk and was half out the door when she stopped me.

"There was one thing..."

"Oh?" I glanced back.

"Molly did confide that she wanted to break up with her boyfriend," Sharon said.

My brows shot up. "Nick?"

Sharon raised one shoulder. "I don't know his name. She was distracted, and I berated her for not keeping her mind on the job. She apologized and said she was worried because she wanted to break up with her boyfriend, and she suspected he would take it badly."

"Did she give a reason why she wanted to break up with him?"

"She said he was too controlling." Sharon turned her attention back to the computer. I thanked her once more before turning to leave, only I tripped over my own feet and jettisoned into the door frame, my head ricocheting off with an audible crack.

"Ow." I cursed, holding a hand to the egg I could already feel forming on my forehead. Sharon was half out of her seat when I held up a hand to stop her.

"Are you all right?" she asked.

"I'm fine. Sorry about that." I waved away her concern. Tripping over my own feet and slamming my head into hard objects was not new for me. I was the clumsiest person I knew.

I left with Ben by my side, peering at my face.

"That one had to have hurt, Fitz," he said. "Look! You've already got a bruise forming!" He poked at my forehead, the icy jab sending a shock through my already traumatized forehead.

I waved him away irritably. "Stop it!" I hissed. "It hurts. The last thing I need is you poking your frozen digit into my brain."

"Right. Sorry." He matched his stride to mine as we left the facility and headed toward my car. "Notice anything?" he asked.

I glanced around. "No? Should I have?"

"We are minus twelve ghosts. You were here a while, plenty of time for them to catch up with you. But they haven't."

I clutched my hands to my chest and barely refrained from a happy dance. "They're gone? They're gone! Oh, happy days, finally, some peace."

"They weren't that much trouble," Ben grumbled, and I wondered if he'd miss them. No idea why. They didn't communicate with him either.

"Not until they started chanting Angel. That was just creepy. But whatever. They're gone now, and I can concentrate on finding out what happened to Molly."

Ben was already in the passenger seat by the time I slid behind the wheel. "What's your next step?" he asked.

"Are you quizzing me?" I demanded, shoving the key in the ignition.

"Whoa, calm down." Ben laughed. "I was just asking what you were going to do next. Out of interest."

"Right. Sorry." Moving the car into reverse, I backed out of my parking space and left Firefly Bay Aged Care Facility in my rearview. "Back to the office to run these names, see what turns up. Call Galloway, see if we have a cause of death yet."

"You're not convinced it was an accident?"

I screwed up my nose while drumming my fingers on the steering wheel. "Usually, I have the victim's ghost to guide me, but since Molly has crossed, I'm flying blind on this one. But according to Galloway, Molly's body was moved. He discovered drag marks from the passenger side of the vehicle to the driver's side. Which means someone was with her in the car. That someone else was driving."

"She wasn't behind the wheel when they found her?"

I shook my head. "No. On the ground outside."

"What do you think happened?"

"That's just it. I have no clue. If it wasn't for Galloway mentioning the drag marks, I'd go with Molly had been driving and attempted to get out of the car after it crashed."

"Except the drag marks say otherwise."

"Exactly. But I didn't really see them. If there had been drag marks, they'd been covered over. I have to trust Galloway's judgment on that one." And given he'd been a detective a lot longer than I'd been a private investigator, I had to believe that Molly had, indeed, been moved after the crash. The big question was, by who?

Chapter Six

Molly's social media revealed hundreds of photos of her and Nick. I scoured the comments for anything racist, any potential threats, or signs that all was not well in their relationship. I found none. There were several photos with another woman, tagged as Angela Brady, Molly's friend from work.

"Angel." The twelve ghosts I thought had departed were crowded in behind me in my office. Their chanting continued, although nowhere near as frequently. I'd semi-successfully managed to tune them out.

"You're getting good at blocking them," Ben said from beside me, where he hovered half in, half out of the desk.

"Yes. Just like I've gotten good at ignoring you standing in the middle of solid objects."

"Sorry." He moved out of the desk to stand behind me, leaning over my shoulder to peer at the screen. "Anything?"

I huffed out a breath. "Nope. Nothing is jumping out at me. Molly and Nick look perfectly happy, but social media is construed that way, isn't it? Everyone is showing their best life when in reality, it's far from the truth."

"True. Is that the friend?" He jabbed at a photo of Molly, Nick, and Angela at a park.

Molly and Nick were smiling at the camera while Angela was looking at Nick.

"That's her." Leaning back in my chair, I pinched the bridge of my nose, a headache starting to throb. That was hardly surprising considering the whack I'd given myself in Sharon's office earlier.

"I'm going to get another coffee. And some pain killers." Standing up, I maneuvered around Ben and headed to the kitchen, leaving him bending over the desk peering at the screen, so close his face was half in and half out. But then, that's how Ben navigated electronic devices by his ghostly touch.

After grabbing a glass of water, I was rummaging around in the drawer for pain killers when Bandit and Thor stampeded inside and thundered down the hallway, cries of, "He's here, he's here" echoing behind them. I glanced at the huge clock on the wall above the sofa. Seven o'clock. The clock had been stuck at seven o'clock for weeks, possibly months because I kept forgetting to get batteries for it. Just like I kept forgetting to charge my smartwatch. But who needed a clock or watch with Bandit and Thor around? They had Galloway's routine down pat. I figured it must be somewhere between five-thirty and six, which was when Galloway typically finished his shift.

Sure enough, the front door opened, and I heard him say, "Hi guys, have a good day?" I smiled to myself as I listened to them fill him in on the goings-on, our new neighbor, Bandit telling him all about Thor puking in my shoe. Of course, Galloway couldn't understand a word of it.

"Babe! What happened?" He'd made it to the open plan living area at the rear of the house with his entourage dancing around his ankles when he saw me at the kitchen bench. Or, more precisely, he saw the bruise on my forehead that stood out like a beacon. The swelling had thankfully receded, only to be replaced by an ugly dark bruise.

I grinned. "The usual. I'm fine."

His long legs ate up the floor, and within seconds, he'd swept me up into his arms and kissed me. And I mean kissed. It was one of those kisses I swooned over in the movies. The way he cupped my face, the way he pulled me flush against his body, the way he projected his love for me in the meeting of our lips. Kade Galloway knew how to kiss!

Slowly easing back, he left his hands looped loosely at my lower back. "I needed that," he whispered.

"Bad day?" I wrapped my arms around his waist and hugged him. "How's Molly's case going?"

He released me and studied my face. "I could ask you the same."

"You know?" I wondered who'd told him.

"Joan Lewis said she'd engaged your services." Ah. Mystery solved.

"She's a grieving mother." I patted his arm in a consoling gesture. "She was pretty angry when she was here. Said the police had told her Molly was drunk driving. Was she?"

Galloway turned his attention to the coffee machine. "Waiting on toxicology and prelim autopsy results," was his noncommittal response.

"Do you still suspect foul play? The drag marks?" I prompted.

He turned and leaned against the counter next to the coffee machine, arms crossed, brow furrowed. "Molly's car had been wiped down."

"Wiped down? As in?"

"As in, no fingerprints," Ben and Galloway said in unison.

"Ben's here," I said for Galloway's benefit, waving absently toward Ben, who was now standing in the middle of the breakfast bar.

"I don't suppose Molly's ghost showed up?" Galloway asked, then added, "Hi, Ben."

"No sign of Molly," I confirmed.

"For the car to be wiped clean of fingerprints, then someone else was definitely in the vehicle," Ben said.

"If someone else was in the vehicle at the time of the crash—" I said.

"Driving. Someone else was driving," Galloway cut in.

"Right. Let's say you're right, and someone else was driving."

"I'm right," Galloway declared.

"Okay, fine. You're right. The point I'm trying to make is that if someone else was driving, wouldn't they be injured?"

Ben silently snapped his fingers and pointed at me. "Good point, Fitz! Were the airbags deployed?"

"Yes." Then I frowned. "But even with the airbags deployed, there'd still be some sort of injury, right? You don't just walk away from an accident like that unscathed. Isn't there bruising from the airbag? Whiplash? Something?"

Galloway was nodding. "And they left the scene. How? On foot? Or was someone else involved? Did someone pick them up?"

I made a mental note to check at the hospital for any admissions that could have been caused by an airbag going off in one's face.

A rapping at the back door followed by, "Hey, Audrey, hi!" had us swiveling to see my new neighbor standing on the back deck, borrowed coffee cup in hand.

Smiling, I hurried to let him in.

"Perfect timing," I said, sliding the door open and gesturing for Seb to come in. "Seb, this is my boyfriend, Kade Galloway. Kade, this is my new neighbor, Seb Castle. Seb's a schoolteacher, third grade."

Seb's white teeth flashed, and he stepped forward, one hand poised to shake Galloway's hand, the other thrusting the coffee cup into my hands. "Great to meet you." Seb shook Galloway's hand with enthusiasm. To me, he added, "Thanks for the coffee, and I'm hoping I'm not too forward, but could I have a refill?"

"Still haven't found your coffee machine?" I could sympathize.

"It's gotta be in one of the boxes, right? Yet I've opened all the ones marked *kitchen,* and it hasn't turned up."

"Why not join us for dinner?" I invited. "We're not doing anything special tonight, are we, babe?"

Galloway took the empty cup from me and moved back to the coffee machine. "By all means, please join us. The more, the merrier."

"I knew the minute I laid eyes on you we were going to be great friends." Seb beamed at me. "Thank you. I'd love to."

"Have a seat." I hopped up onto a stool at the breakfast bar and patted the one next to me. Seb sat.

"Are you cooking, or are we ordering in? Cos if it's the latter, I'm happy to chip in. In fact, my treat."

"Oh, I don't cook all that often. The kitchen is more Galloway's domain than mine."

Seb chuckled. "Good to know. So, you two live together?"

I shook my head. "Nah, it's just me, Thor, and Bandit. Galloway has his own place."

"For now," Galloway added. He'd finished at the coffee machine, turning with two cups and placing them in front of Seb and me. I shot him a look, caught by surprise. We'd never even talked about moving in together. Did Galloway have plans I didn't know about? Not that I had any complaints, it was just that life had been so busy ever since Ben died that I'd never really thought about the next steps. The next logical steps. You know the ones—moving in together, getting engaged, getting hitched, having babies.

A cold shiver shot down my spine that was not ghost-related. Witnessing the birth of my niece had put the brakes on any baby-making plans. Even my ovaries had gone silent, which was telling. I'd always thought I'd have kids one day, but now? Now I wasn't so sure. Galloway had reassured me all was well and that it didn't matter if I didn't want kids, but looking at him now, I couldn't help but wonder. Did he? Was he ready to settle down and start a family? I swallowed. Was I ready?

"So, Audrey tells me you're a cop?" Seb's voice broke into my thoughts.

Galloway inclined his head. "Detective."

"I'd love to set something up, have you come in and talk with the kids about your work," Seb gushed, leaning forward on his elbows.

"Elementary school is a little early for career planning, isn't it?" Galloway quirked a brow and took a sip of his drink.

"It's never too early. And usually, we do get the police in—at least we did in the city—to chat with the kids but typically not a detective. I think the kids would love it."

Galloway shrugged and muttered a noncommittal, "We'll see. I don't feel like cooking tonight, so I suggest pizza." He changed the subject. Luckily, pizza was one of my favorite topics.

"Yum. I'm in." I beamed.

Seb was already pulling out his wallet. "I'm in, and I'm paying."

"No need. I've got this." Galloway had his phone out and was punching in our order. "We use the app. It's connected to my credit card."

Seb's face fell. "Oh. Okay then. Well, I owe you one." He turned to me. "I remember when we used to have to phone our orders in and then pay in cash when the delivery guy arrived."

I laughed. "Right? I feel a million years old when I say this, but I can't keep up with all the apps. There's one for everything, or so it seems."

"They'll be delivering pizzas by drones next."

"Aren't they already doing that?" Galloway asked. "Maybe not pizzas—not yet—but some companies are using drones to deliver to their customers."

"Driverless cars," I added.

"Wonder how Castle would handle that," Seb said, and Galloway and I looked at him, confused.

"What do you mean?" I asked.

"Oh, sorry!" Seb blushed. "I do that sometimes. Just like you talk to yourself, I catch myself asking what Castle would do."

I frowned, even more confused. "Aren't you Castle? Seb Castle?" Had I gotten his name wrong, and he'd been too polite to correct me?

Seb laughed. "Yes, I'm Seb Castle. You didn't get it wrong." He read my mind. "No, I meant Richard Castle. The crime-writing author who teams up with—"

"Detective Kate Becket!" I declared, clutching his arm. "I love that show!"

Seb lit up. "You do? Me too. Of course, it helps that Richard and I share a surname."

"That's so cool."

"Really, Fitz?" Ben drawled, shaking his head at me. "It's hardly cool that Seb shares the same last name as a fictional television character."

"Shush, you." I waved him away, turning my attention back to Seb, who was now looking at me in what could only be described as a confused fashion.

Ben burst into peals of laughter while I tried to regroup. "Sorry. Not you. I thought Galloway was going to say something smart, and I was pre-empting it," I lied, then shot Galloway an apologetic look, praying he'd play along.

He did because he's awesome like that.

"She does that a lot too," he offered with an indulgent smile, then leaned across the breakfast bar to drop an affectionate kiss on the tip of my nose. I beamed at him. He really was the best—and hottest—boyfriend in the entire world.

Dinner passed in a blur of too much pizza, just enough wine, and reminiscing about our favorite episodes of *Castle*. We'd just cleared the table when Galloway's phone dinged.

"Man, I'm beat." Seb stretched and yawned, carrying his wine glass to the sink and rinsing it out before leaving it to drain. "I'm going to head off. Thanks so much for dinner. I owe you guys one. I mean it. We'll set something up once I get everything unpacked."

"Come on over in the morning for a coffee," I invited, following him to the back door.

"You sure?"

"Of course. Have a good night." I waved goodbye, sliding the door shut behind him. Galloway had murmured an absent-minded goodbye, his attention on his phone.

"What's up?" I asked, sliding my arm around his waist.

"Prelim autopsy report for Molly just came in," he said, wiggling the phone.

"Oooh!" I craned my neck to get a look. "What does it say?"

"She died from a tension pneumothorax."

"What's that?"

"Broken ribs punctured her lung."

"Ouch." I absently rubbed my hand up and down Galloway's spine.

"Seatbelt bruising confirms Molly was in the passenger seat at the time of impact."

"You were right. She *was* moved."

"And the ME thinks that whoever moved her, that's when the broken ribs punctured her lung. That if they'd left her where she was, she'd still be alive today."

"So, we're talking…"

"A manslaughter charge," he said, voice grim.

"And tox?"

"While she did have alcohol in her system, she wasn't intoxicated. The toxicology report also showed a sedative."

"Wait! You're saying someone slipped a sedative in her drink, shoved her into the passenger seat of her car, crashed that car, then attempted to make it look like Molly had been the one driving? Intentionally. So, not manslaughter? We're looking at murder." It wasn't a question.

Galloway nodded grimly, then pulled me close, cradling me against his chest. I snuggled in with a sigh before a yawn overtook me.

"Come on, let's go to bed. We'll tackle this with fresh eyes in the morning."

Probably a good idea. I wasn't sure how sharp I'd be with my belly full of pizza and my mind scrambled with wine.

There is nothing like the sound of a cat puking to wake you from a deep sleep.

"Thor!" I bolted upright, threw the covers off, and launched out of bed, only my foot wasn't clear of the covers, and I fell, one leg tangled in the bed sheets, darn near ripping my leg off.

"Oof." I face-planted on the carpet, my hip screaming in agony while I tried to push myself back onto the bed.

"Audrey?" Galloway's voice was rough with sleep.

"I'm fine," I whispered. Goodness knows why I was whispering. It wasn't like I hadn't already woken him up.

"What are you doing?" He flicked on the bedside lamp and looked at me, dangling half off the bed.

"I heard Thor vomiting," I whispered. "I thought I could get to him before... anyway.

Needless to say, I got tangled up, and now I'm stuck."

Galloway shook his head. "Here." He grabbed my wrist and hauled me back onto the bed. "You okay? Did you hurt yourself?"

My hip throbbed. "No," I lied with a fake smile, hoping he wouldn't notice my watering eyes in the dim light.

"You want me to go?" he offered.

"No, I've got it. You go back to sleep." Swiveling, I lowered both legs to the floor. I stood, taking exaggerated steps to ensure I didn't inadvertently trip over thin air. The more I moved, the less my hip hurt. By the time I'd made it downstairs, I was pain-free. Kinda.

"Thor?" I hissed, searching for my overweight vomiting feline.

"What?" he replied, waddling down the hallway.

"Was that you?"

"Was that me, what?"

I rolled my eyes. He was being deliberately obtuse.

"Was that you puking? Where is it? You'd better not have vomited in my shoes again."

"They're the perfect receptacle," he protested. "Would you prefer I vomit all over the floor? Surely that's harder to clean up."

"I'd prefer not to be cleaning it up at all," I grumbled, following him into the living area. "Can't you take it outside? Vomit on the lawn? What's making you sick anyway, Thor? I'm starting to get worried. Maybe I do need to take you back to the vet."

"Oh, no." He shook his head. "Nuh-uh, no way. I refuse."

"Seems we're at an impasse then," I grumbled, spying a pair of shoes I'd toed off and left by the back door. "You don't want to go to the vet, and I don't want you vomiting."

Sure enough, one shoe, the left one to be precise, was now home to cat barf. Picking it up, I opened the back door and tossed it outside. I'd deal with it in the morning. Bandit, who'd followed me downstairs, jumped onto the sofa, watching us.

"What do you know about this?" I asked her. "What's making Thor sick?"

"I don't know, Mom," she said solemnly. Knowing how Thor had the raccoon wrapped around his paw, I doubted she'd tell me, even if she knew. But then sometimes Bandit was a little too naïve for her own good and would spill his secrets by accident.

I crossed the room and squatted in front of her, scratching her ears.

"Keep an eye on him for me, okay?" I whispered. "I'm worried about him. If he's eating something he shouldn't, it just might kill him." Her whole body stiffened, and I ran a soothing hand over her fur. I didn't think Thor was on death's door, but I was concerned. Maybe Thor was protesting his diet by making himself sick. I wouldn't put it past him. But it wouldn't hurt to have Bandit think Thor was in danger and be my little spy.

"Okay," she whispered.

"Good girl." I dropped a kiss on her head and headed back upstairs to bed.

Chapter Seven

"Why is your shoe on the back lawn?" Ben asked the following morning.

"Cat barf," I replied, half asleep at the coffee machine.

Ben sighed and shook his head. "What is it with that cat?"

"Don't worry, I'm on it," I reassured him. I figured Bandit would soon dish the dirt on what Thor was getting into that was making him sick. If not, it was off to the vet we'd go.

Ben turned his attention from the back lawn to me. "What's on the agenda for today?"

"We looked at Molly's social media yesterday and didn't turn up anything interesting. Can you check Nick's?"

"You think he's the one who's responsible for Molly's death?"

"I didn't see any sign of injury when I spoke with him yesterday, but then, I wasn't looking for it. No, I want to check his alibi. He said he was in the city visiting his sick grandmother. I want to confirm he wasn't in Firefly Bay the night Molly died."

"Sure, I can do that. What are you going to do?"

"I'm going to visit Angela Brady. That photo of the three of them in the park is niggling at me. In particular, the way Angela was looking at Nick."

"Angel," my twelve ghosts chanted, and I pinched the bridge of my nose, pushing down the wave of irritation their presence aroused. I'd barely slept after Thor had woken me with his vomiting. Instead, I'd laid in bed and thought about Molly. Who had wanted to kill her, and why? The ghosts had chanted all night long, making sleep impossible. Galloway had risen early and was long gone by the time I finally dragged myself out of bed, and now I was sleep-deprived and in no mood for a bunch of ghosts who wouldn't tell me why they were haunting me.

"Shush!" I snapped at them.

"Angel," they responded, even louder. Tipping my head back, I stared at the ceiling, praying for strength. A tap at the back door had me swiveling my neck so fast it made a loud cracking noise. Great. Now I had a sore neck to add to my aching hip.

"Morning!" Seb smiled his thousand-watt smile and waved at me through the glass.

"Right," I muttered under my breath. "I forgot I'd invited him over for coffee this morning."

"Just tell him now's not a good time," Ben said.

"It's fine. I'll make him a coffee, and he can go. He's got things to do anyway, like unpacking."

I slid open the door, and Seb eyed me up and down. "Urgh. You look rough. Bad night?"

"Couldn't sleep." I waved at the coffee machine. "Help yourself. I'm going to take a shower and get dressed. Sorry, I can't hang out. I've got work."

"That's fine. I can't linger either. I really need to find my coffee machine, finish unpacking, then I need to check-in at school."

"On a Saturday?"

"Yeah, got a meeting with the principal. Said he needed me for something before I officially start on Monday."

I was already walking toward the hallway, not really listening. "Sure. Have a good day."

"You too, Audrey."

Standing under the shower, I shut my eyes and let the hot water revive me. I had a feeling today was going to include a nap somewhere along the line, but first, I needed to find out what happened to Molly. I made myself a mental checklist. Ben was set to check Nick's alibi, see if he really was in the city. I would interview her best friend, Angela, then I'd have to give Molly's mom a call and update her on the case. But first, I should check in with Galloway just in case there was anything he didn't want Joan Lewis to know. Not that Joan was a suspect. I highly doubted she killed her own daughter. I paused. Was that a reason to rule her out? Just because she was the parent of the deceased. Heck, no. I added her to my list of suspects.

Re-energized, I dressed, dropped a kiss on Thor's and Bandit's respective furry heads as they both slept on my bed, then hurried downstairs. Ben was in the office, his hand resting on top of my computer.

"How's it going?"

"A lot to sift through. I'm starting with social media, but I want to see if I can get into his emails and messages as well."

"You can do that?"

"I can try. I can follow the electronic data, so there's no reason I can't follow the email address he uses to sign in. As long as I have an entry point, I should be okay."

"I'm off to see Angela. Let me know if you find anything."

"Will do. And Fitz?"

"Yeah?"

"You are aware that you're wearing two different shoes, right?"

"What?" I glanced down at my feet. Sure enough. One red shoe, one blue. I ran upstairs, fixed my shoe situation, ran back down, called goodbye to Ben, and headed out.

Ben had found Angela's address for me the night before, and as I approached her apartment, I spotted her standing in the doorway talking to a man.

"We're done," Angela said with a sniff and a toss of her hair. "C'est la vie. You're going to miss me but believe this—I don't need you. I'm not going to sit at home and cry for you."

"Angie," the man said, reaching a hand toward her.

She slapped it away. "Go home to your wife, Dean."

My eyes rounded, and I paused, taking in the scene before me. Angela Brady was having an affair with a married man! Correction. She *had* been having an affair; now she was dumping him, and I had a front-row seat.

Angela noticed me. And glared. "Yes?" she snapped. "What do you want?"

I straightened my spine and took a step forward. "Audrey Fitzgerald, Delaney Investigations," I introduced myself. "I'm here about Molly."

Angela's face fell, and her eyes welled with tears. The man she'd just dumped turned, and I caught a glimpse of his pale face before he shoved past me and hurried away. That's when I noticed what he was wearing. Underneath the coat was a uniform. Like a nurse would wear. Like I'd seen the staff at Firefly Bay's Residential Aged Care Facility wearing. Did he work there?

"Who was that?" I asked Angela.

"None of your business." She sniffed, wiping her nose on her sleeve. "You'd better come in. I've given the neighbors enough to talk about today." She stood back, and I dutifully stepped inside. I figured Angela was a minimalist, for her apartment was bare, almost barren. No knick-knacks, only functional furniture, all in white to match the walls. Even the rug in front of the sofa was white, and I couldn't help but think what a pain it would be to keep clean. It was open plan, like my house, only on a much smaller scale.

"Nice place," I said. My ghostly entourage followed me inside, but they wouldn't all fit, so they were half in and half out of the walls. I ignored them. After their night of chanting, they were blissfully silent for a change.

"You said you were here about Molly?" Angela pointed to a seat at the round dining table. "Sit."

I dutifully sat, watching as she moved around in the kitchen, her movements fluid, elegant. She didn't seem to notice she'd walked through at least three ghosts on her trek from the refrigerator to the cupboard to get a glass.

"Juice?" she offered.

"Coffee?" I asked hopefully.

"I don't drink hot drinks." She poured herself a glass of orange juice and joined me at the table while I tried to get my head around what it would be like to not only not drink coffee but not drink hot drinks at all. I couldn't begin to imagine it.

"So?" she said sharply.

"So?" I repeated, puzzled.

"About Molly?" I could hear the irritation in her voice.

"Right, yes, sorry. So, tell me about your relationship with Molly. You were friends?"

"Yes."

I blinked. Okay. Angela Brady was going to be a tough nut to crack. "Where did you meet? Have you been friends for long?"

"We met at work."

"Oh! So, you haven't been friends for long?" I'd assumed she and Molly had been friends since childhood.

She rolled her shoulders. "A year or so, I guess."

"And did you hang out outside of work?"

She nodded. "Sure."

"When was the last time you saw Molly?"

Angela looked up at the ceiling, thinking. "Um. I haven't seen her in a while. We're on different shifts. She's on days. I'm on nights. I may have caught a glimpse of her during shift change, but we haven't hung out for a while."

"And why's that?"

Her green eyes flashed. "Night shift. Day shift," she repeated.

"Yes, but you're not both at work all the time," I said. "Weekends?"

"We were both busy outside of work. Molly had Nick. I had..." She trailed off, clamping her lips together in a firm line.

"What did you think of Molly and Nick? Were they solid?"

She cocked her head. "I guess."

It was my turn to frown. "So, Molly didn't tell you she wanted to end things with him?"

Angela's eyebrows shot up in surprise. "First I've heard of it. Who told you that?"

"Sharon Mooney. Your boss."

Angela snorted. "She's a busybody who thrives on gossip. I wouldn't believe a word she says. Nosy old cow."

"Molly would have confided in you, wouldn't she, if things were bad between her and Nick?"

She bit her lip. "Maybe. Once upon a time, yes. Now, I'm not so sure."

"Why's that?"

Angela deflated in her chair. Her shoulders rolled forward, and she slumped, chin to chest. "She found out about me and..." She trailed off, clamping her lips shut.

"That guy?" I jerked my head toward the front door. "You work with him, right?"

"Yeah." She blew out a breath. "Okay, you're probably going to find out anyway since the cops are poking around too. I've been having an affair with Dean Ackerman. He's an RN at work. Molly found out and threatened to tell Dean's wife. Molly disapproves of that sort of thing. Cheating. She was very moral. Yet it didn't seem to bother her none stealing Nick away from me." She finished on a bitter note.

"You and Nick were an item?" What a shocker. I hadn't picked up on that at all. There was that one photo on social media where Angela was looking at Nick rather intently. Still, I wouldn't have said it was with longing or desire.

Angela was shaking her head. "No. We never went out. But Molly knew I liked him. I'd made a couple of passes at him, and he'd turned me down."

"Wow. That must've been awkward."

She shrugged. "There are plenty more fish in the sea."

"Right. So, Nick turned you down, then started going out with Molly. And you started a relationship with a married man."

"That's about it."

"You said he—Dean Ackerman—is an RN? Like Sharon?"

"Yes."

"So, he's your boss? You report to him?"

Her lips thinned. "We don't have a set boss. Molly and I are certified nursing assistants. We report to any registered nurse on duty."

"And both Sharon Mooney and Dean Ackerman are registered nurses?" I persisted.

"Correct."

I blinked, digesting this news. Was it against protocol for an RN to be in a relationship with a subordinate? I had no idea, but I'd look into it. It was definitely against protocol for a married man to have an affair with a colleague, though. And Molly knew.

"How did Molly find out?" I asked.

"She caught us. At work." Angela studied her nails as if the entire subject was tedious, yet I saw the way her leg was jiggling under the table. She was nervous.

"Eek. That couldn't have been good."

"It wasn't. I'm not sure who she was angrier at, me or Dean. Possibly Dean because he was the married one."

"And he's your superior at work," I pointed out again.

"That too."

"What did Molly say? When she busted you."

"She waved a finger in Dean's face and told him he should be ashamed of himself. And that if we didn't cut it out immediately, she'd tell Katherine. His wife."

"What did Dean say?"

"He said that it wouldn't happen again."

"And did it? Happen again?"

"Oh yes, many times. Dean is very good at lying to your face and telling you what you want to hear."

"Did Molly have an ultimatum for you?"

There was a moment's silence as Angela studied me. I'm not sure what she saw. An exhausted PI with dark circles under her eyes? Or a tenacious investigator who was determined to get to the truth. Both fit.

"She told me she'd report me."

"To Sharon?"

Angela snorted. "That would be pointless. No. She threatened to go higher up, to the Director of Nursing. We could lose our jobs."

"They'd fire you?"

"Oh, not outright. I'd either be performance managed out the door, or my shifts would be drastically cut, forcing me to leave to find another job."

"Right." I nodded. "So, you ended things with Dean. That's what I just witnessed."

But Angela shook her head. "Nah. Apparently, I have a problem with authority. As soon as someone tells me I can't do something, I do it. Or say they want me to dump my boyfriend? I double down."

Now I was confused. "But that was him, right? Did I not just witness you dumping him?"

"Yeah. All of this happened with Molly a couple of weeks ago. Nothing really changed after she caught us. We kept sneaking around."

"Why did you break things off with him then if it wasn't because of Molly catching you?"

She waved a hand in the air. "I was just bored of it. At first, it was fun. Hot. Sexy and sinful. But lately, all I'm hearing is Dean complaining about his bad back and his paranoia that his wife is going to find out."

"If he was so worried about his wife finding out, why didn't he end it?"

"Because he has no balls." Angela scoffed. "To be honest, he's a demon in the sack but outside of it? Absolute wimp. Gutless. That eventually got to be a drag. Took all the fun out of it, so I ended things."

She finished her juice and stood, stretching. "Is that all? I hardly think Molly's accident warrants a private investigator or that my love life has any bearing." She turned her back, rinsing the glass at the sink.

"Oh, Molly's death wasn't accidental." I stood, digging in my bag for a business card. "Someone set it up to make the police think that."

Angela stood frozen at the sink before slowly turning her head to look at me over her shoulder, her face devoid of color. "Someone..." She choked, then cleared her throat and tried again. "Someone *killed* her? On purpose?"

I bit my lip. Maybe I shouldn't have told her that, but it was too late now. The cat was out of the bag. I inclined my head. "Yes." I tapped the business card I'd just placed on the table. "If you think of anything, call me."

I was at the front door when she called out. "Wait!"

"Yes?" I paused, hand on the doorknob.

"You didn't ask me if I thought anyone wanted Molly dead," she said.

"Do you?"

"No."

"Well… if you think of anyone, let me know." I let myself out.

Chapter Eight

"We have a problem," Ben greeted me when I returned home. I vetoed the office for the coffee machine, sorely in need.

"Oh, what about?"

"I can't confirm Nick's alibi."

I paused for a micro-second. "That's not like you. What's up?"

"I can only track electronic meta-data."

"Yes, I know. What's the problem?" I didn't pause in my coffee making preparations. Fatigue was nipping at my heels, and I really needed a pick me up. Wait, that's a lie. What I really needed was a nap.

"So, Nick said he was visiting his grandmother. Only a little digging reveals she has dementia, and she's in palliative care in a nursing home. They don't have CCTV, and they don't have an electronic sign-in system," Ben said, reminding me that we were still talking about the case and not debating the merits of a nap over coffee.

"Surely we can trace his steps in the city somehow?"

"You know how big the city is? How much data I'd have to trawl through? I thought about getting into the traffic cams and searching for his car, but it's a longshot."

Coffee made, I took a sip, pondering. "Okay. If Grandma is in a home, Nick wouldn't be staying with her like I'd initially assumed. He probably booked a hotel."

"I've checked all of the ones within a ten-mile radius. He's not registered in any of them."

"Damn. Okay, so, what's your next move?"

"I'm going to check the local hostel. We're forgetting Nick is a student. He probably can't afford to stay at a hotel. We're talking budget backpacker type accommodation."

"Okay, that makes sense." I slipped off my shoes and rubbed my aching feet. "We have to find the motivation for Nick to kill Molly. All we have is an unsubstantiated rumor that she wanted to break things off with him. Hardly a reason to kill her."

A rap on the back door startled me, and I let out a little squeak, pivoting toward the door. Seb stood there, holding the coffee cup he'd borrowed earlier.

"Hey." He waved.

"If this keeps up, it's going to be a problem," Ben said, crossing his arms over his chest. I had flashbacks of my previous neighbor, Mrs. Hill, and her almost busting me talking to a ghost. Multiple times.

"Hi, Seb. Found your coffee pot yet?" I asked, opening the door and waving him inside.

"Yes!" He beamed. "It was in a bathroom box. Wrapped in towels."

"Excellent."

"So, is that how you work your cases?" he asked, shoving the cup he was holding toward me. "I'm returning this," he added.

My brow furrowed. "What do you mean?" I took the cup and set it on the breakfast bar.

"Pacing back and forth talking to yourself. You were even pointing at one point. Almost like someone else is here, and you're talking to them."

My eyes widened in alarm. "How long were you standing there?"

"Oh, God, now I seem like a stalker!" He barked out a laugh and slapped my upper arm. "Sorry, I wasn't spying, honest. I was only there for about a minute. You were so engrossed that I was loathe to interrupt."

"Right."

"I see there's another shoe on the lawn. Still having trouble with Thor?"

The thing with Seb Castle was that not only was he good to look at, but he was also very charismatic to boot. The problem with that was if he found out I could talk to ghosts, could I trust him to keep it a secret? Or would my talent be fodder for the gossip mill?

"Yeah."

"I have a suggestion for you that might help," he offered.

"Really?" That piqued my interest.

"Thor is on a diet because he's overweight, yeah? So, how about getting him a little more active, to burn off a few of those calories, and then the food intake won't be such an issue."

Ben snorted. "How do you get a cat to exercise?"

I chuckled. "Right?"

"What?" Seb said.

"Sorry. I meant, how would I get Thor to exercise?"

"The red dot. Get yourself a laser pointer, spend a few minutes a day playing with it. If Thor is like every other cat in the universe, he'll chase that thing until he collapses of exhaustion."

"I'm not sure I want that to happen," I protested.

"Well, no, obviously don't do that. Start off slow. A minute a day and build up. Bandit would probably enjoy it too."

"You know, that's not a bad idea," Ben said, nodding.

I echoed his words.

"Happy to help." Seb flashed those pearly whites again. "In return, I was hoping you could help me."

"Oh?"

"Another favor already?" Ben crossed his arms over his chest, legs planted. "This guy has balls." I wanted to point out the obvious —that yes, Seb is male; therefore, he does indeed have balls—but held my tongue.

"So, I checked in with the school, and tomorrow night is the junior school dance, and I've been scheduled to chaperone. Would you be my date?"

I blinked. *A date?* "You know I have a boyfriend, right?" I hedged. Seb was great, and I liked him as a *friend*. I had zero intentions of dating the guy!

Seb grinned. "I don't see a ring on it." He winked.

"Oh, he didn't!" Ben declared, arms dropping to his sides, mouth agape.

"He did." I shook my head in disbelief.

"What?" It was Seb's turn to frown. "Come on, seriously, is there someone else here? Do you have an earpiece, and you're talking to someone? That's it, isn't it?"

"Sorry, can't reveal trade secrets." His reasoning wasn't bad, actually. I could pretend I was using surveillance equipment and someone, aka Ben, was talking to me. That would totally work.

"You're a pretty cool chick, Audrey Fitzgerald." Seb's cocky grin was back, and while I was relieved my ghost talking abilities hadn't scared him off—yet—that didn't mean I wanted him getting the wrong idea about him and me.

"I meant what I said, Seb. I'm with Galloway, and I love him very much. I've no intentions of going on a date with you." I did my best to let him down gently, still surprised that he'd even asked, especially considering he already knew about Galloway and me.

Seb blinked for a second, his face blank, then he threw back his head and roared with laughter. Ben and I looked from each other to Seb, who was doubled over, holding his belly and laughing up a storm. I shifted from one foot to the other, my patience slipping. Was he laughing at *me*?

"I fail to see what's so funny," I eventually grumbled.

Seb sobered, wiping his fingers beneath his eyes. "Sorry." He chuckled, composing himself. "Sorry," he repeated, clearing his throat, visibly straightening his spine, and rolling his shoulders back.

"When I said date, I didn't mean... *date*."

"What did you mean? Exactly," I deadpanned.

"I'm new in town, and you're pretty much the only person I know. I thought it'd be fun to do something together, and since I'm supposed to chaperone the dance, you could come with. Heck, bring Kade too. In fact, that's an excellent idea." The way his voice dropped when he said Galloway's name and his eyes took on a dreamy quality had me cocking my head.

"Are you gay?" I asked bluntly.

"Oh, he's gay," Ben agreed, arms back across his chest, head nodding. "You see the way he got all dark and brooding when you mentioned Galloway?"

"Yeah," I nodded. "Didn't pick up on it earlier, though."

"Me either."

"You're definitely talking to someone!" Seb accused, glancing around.

"Stop dodging the question!" I shot back. "Look, just in case it matters, I don't mind. I don't care if you're gay, bi, trans, alien, a ghost, whatever."

"Alien?" Seb laughed. "Really?"

I narrowed my eyes. "Are you?" Would I care if he was an alien? No. I'd be extremely curious, though.

Seb shook his head and ran a hand around the back of his neck, a rueful grin twisting his lips. "I'm gay. You got me."

My eyes widened. "Are you, you know, not out yet?"

"Oh, I'm out. Have been since I was a teenager. I just didn't want my arrival in a small country town to be about my sexuality."

"Firefly Bay is hardly a small country town." I sniffed indignantly.

"Yeah, it is," Ben said.

"Compared to the city, it is," Seb said.

Fair point. I wasn't going to quibble on semantics.

"Your secret is safe with me," I assured him. "Let me get back to you on the dance." I'd run it by Galloway and see what he thought. "Although a school dance on a Sunday? Is that new?"

Seb huffed out a sigh. "Weird, right? Turns out they had to cancel it earlier. Something about a water leak in the gym. Due to a *very busy school and social activity calendar,*" he air quoted, "they had to squeeze the junior dance in on a Sunday or make them wait until the end of next term. The committee voted and agreed a Sunday was fine, and I got thrown under the bus for chaperoning."

Probably because he's the new guy, I thought. I couldn't see any of the other teachers voting for a school activity on the weekend.

"I have an idea." Ben nudged me, sending an icy blast into my rib cage. I hissed in a breath and stepped away. "What?" I whispered as if Seb weren't standing right in front of me, watching with those piercing blue eyes of his.

"Why are we whispering?" Seb whispered, glancing out the back window before bringing his gaze back to me. "Is someone here? Are we in danger?"

"Danger?" I blurted. "No!"

"Okay, something is going on with you. I've told you my secret, now spill. I promise I won't tell a soul. Scout's honor." He crossed himself, revealing he was no boy scout, and despite myself, I liked that about him. In fact, I liked everything about Sebastian Castle. He reminded me a little of Ben, only a blond and much better-looking version.

"You can't tell anyone," I warned, seriously considering telling him the truth.

"Fitz!" Ben warned. "No way. Do not tell him. Let me do some recon first, for heaven's sake. Just because he told you he's gay does not mean you have to tell him about your ghost whispering abilities."

I chewed my lip. Ben was right. What if I told him, and he either didn't believe me or he did but couldn't keep his mouth shut? That would be disastrous.

I pointed to my ear. "I'm testing out my new surveillance equipment." The lie rolled off my tongue with ease.

Seb stepped toward me and spoke directly into my ear. "Is that you, Kade?" To me, he said, "It's your boyfriend, isn't it?"

I shook my head. "Actually, it's not. It's a friend of mine. Ben."

"Shh, don't tell him any more," Ben hissed. "You already told him my name is Ben. Do not give him my surname."

"Gotcha."

"Right." Seb stepped back, nodding. "That's really good. I can't even see it!"

I held up my thumb and forefinger in a pinching motion. "Really small."

"It's amazing what they can do these days. Does Ben want to come to the school dance?"

"Hah!" Ben snorted. "A school dance? Pass. Pretty sure the school didn't intend for their new teacher to invite half the neighborhood along as chaperones either."

"Ah, that would be a no thanks." I smiled politely at Seb, then turned when I heard a ding from my office. An email had arrived.

"Sorry, I need to check that. It could be about my case," I said, heading for my office. Seb didn't take the hint to leave. Instead, he trailed behind, following me.

The email was from the Ivelisse Day Spa with a ten percent discount voucher if I booked a treatment this month. As I closed the email, I heard the Little Mix song, *Black Magic*, again. Faint, but definitely there. "Do you hear that?" I asked.

"Hear what?" Seb asked. He was leaning against the doorframe of my office, a pose so similar to Ben's that my heart ached.

"Music."

Seb shook his head. "Nope. Nothing. So..." He pushed away from the doorframe and stepped inside. "This is where it all happens, huh?"

I nodded and spun in my chair. "Not all of it. A lot of it is out and about, interviewing people, chasing down leads, that type of thing."

Seb paused to study my murder board. On it were pictures of Molly and potential suspects. He tapped Molly's photo. "This is your victim?"

I decided it wouldn't hurt to talk the case through with him. It wasn't like he knew any of them.

"Yes, Molly Lewis, twenty-one, a nurse assistant at the local aged care facility. Died in a car accident." I tapped Nick's photo. "Her boyfriend, Nick Davidson, uni-student and burger flipper." I tapped

Angela's photo. "Molly's best friend, Angela Brady. Also co-worker." It reminded me that my board needed updating. "I need to add in Angela's ex-boyfriend, Dean Ackerman, who is one of her bosses at the aged care facility and a married man. Apparently, Molly found out about their affair and was threatening to tell Dean's wife."

"You think he, or she," Seb pointed to Dean and Angela, "killed Molly to keep her quiet."

I chewed the inside of my cheek. "It's motive. But I need to check alibis."

"And the boyfriend?" Seb turned his attention back to Nick's photo. "Does he have a motive? And an alibi?"

"I'm working on it. Molly's boss told me that Molly wanted to break up with Nick, but I haven't confirmed it. When I spoke with Nick, they hadn't broken up. And he has an alibi. He was in the city visiting his sick grandmother the night Molly died."

"In the city?" Seb was tapping his chin and moving his head from one side to the other as he studied Nick's face. "He looks awfully familiar."

My eyebrows shot into my hairline. "You know him? You know Nick Davidson?"

Seb shook his head. "Don't know the name, sorry, but his face… I'm pretty sure I've seen him before. That hair and that bone structure tend to stand out."

"You're saying you remember some black kid with long hair that you may have walked past in the city?" I was incredulous. Nick was all sharp angles, but it wasn't enough to make me remember him if I'd passed him in the street.

Seb chuckled. "Not in the city in general, but I may have seen him in a nightclub I frequent."

I gasped. "A gay nightclub? Are you saying Nick Davidson is gay?"

Seb held up both hands. "I'm not saying that at all! I'm saying I think I may have seen this guy at The Manor. It might not even be him. And he may not be gay. Believe it or not, straight people frequent gay bars."

"Right, yes, of course. I know better than to jump to conclusions."

"Do you, though?" Ben drawled. He'd been watching our exchange from the doorway. I shot him an irritated frown, then jerked my head toward the computer. Seb had just narrowed our search considerably. If it was Nick Davidson he'd seen at The Manor, then Ben could check their CCTV footage and get confirmation.

"Well," I swung my arms by my side and smiled brightly at Seb, "thanks for the intel. I'm going to get cracking on following up on that, so..." I trailed off.

"So, get out so you can get to work?" Seb finished, flashing his teeth in a cheeky grin.

"Pretty much."

"Okay, Audrey Fitzgerald, I'll leave you to it." He leaned in until his mouth was practically touching my ear. "See you, Ben!"

"See ya," Ben answered absently, his hand submerged in my computer as he searched for evidence on Nick's movements in the city.

"He says bye," I offered. "I'll let you know about the dance."

Chapter Nine

"What did you do?" Joan Lewis stormed along the sidewalk in front of Nick's place, hair disheveled, her face wrought with despair. "Molly's dead, and you killed her!"

I'd managed to catch up with Nick as he was leaving his house, and we were standing next to his hunk o' junk car when Joan turned up, full of fury and pain.

"Don't be stupid," Nick replied. "I loved Molly."

The slap snapped his head back, the sound loud and harsh.

"Hey!" I protested, stepping in between them, one hand on Nick's chest, the other held out toward Joan, warning her off. "There's no need for that."

"My girl is lying in the mortuary. Do you think it's funny?" Joan screeched. "Molly died. A car accident. Only she wasn't driving." Okay, so the police had told her about that. Now she was a momma bear on the warpath.

"It wasn't me! I wouldn't hurt her, I swear!" Nick pleaded.

"Please, Mrs. Lewis, this isn't helping." I wrapped my arm around the other woman's shoulders and steered her away from Nick. "Let the police deal with this, okay?"

"He killed my daughter." She sniffed. "He can't be allowed to get away with it."

"Nick wasn't in Firefly Bay the night she died," I said.

"He's lying. She said she was seeing him that night," Joan insisted.

That may have been what Molly told her mom, but it wasn't the truth, and I had the evidence to back it up. Not that Joan wanted to hear any of it.

"What's going on here?" Galloway pulled up beside us, engine rumbling, window rolled down, elbow resting on the car door.

"Mrs. Lewis was just leaving," I assured him, casting a glance toward Nick, where he stood on the sidewalk staring at us.

"I hope you're here to arrest him," she spat, shooting Nick one last hateful glare before returning to her car, a car I hadn't noticed tailing me—and I should have, considering she'd pulled in right behind me.

"You told her he was a suspect?" Galloway raised a brow.

"Nope. As far as she's concerned, Nick Davidson killed her daughter. She told me that the second she hired me."

"And you believe her?"

"Actually, no."

"Oh? Why's that?"

"Because he has a solid alibi." I leaned down, resting my forearms on the roof of the car, and told him what we'd discovered.

"Is that right?" Galloway tapped the steering wheel with his thumb. "Maybe we should go talk with him, eh?"

I nodded. "That had been my intention before Joan turned up." It wasn't a coincidence Galloway had turned up when he did either. He was here to talk to Nick just like I was.

"Got any idea who Molly might have been with the night she died?" Galloway asked Nick after parking his car and joining us on the sidewalk.

"Not a clue," Nick said, jaw rigid.

"Why didn't you say you were at The Manor?" Galloway asked.

"What?" Nick glanced from Galloway to me and back again.

"We've seen CCTV footage. We can place you there," I added.

"We know what type of club that is, Nick," Galloway continued. "We know you were there the night Molly died."

"My family doesn't know." Nick grimaced, shooting a glance toward the house. The house he lived in with his parents. "Please don't tell them. They'll kill me."

"We're not going to tell your family," Galloway assured him. "Let's start again, shall we? With the truth this time?"

"I was at The Manor until around four," Nick admitted, scuffing his foot on the sidewalk.

"Did Molly know you were gay?" I asked.

"She was the only one in Firefly Bay who guessed," he said. "She said she'd be my beard. You know, make it look like I was straight."

"Why?"

"She wanted a cover story too. She was seeing someone."

"Who?"

"I dunno, she wouldn't say." Picking up the backpack at his feet, he swung it over his shoulder. "Can I go now? I got work."

"Sure." Galloway waved him away, then slung his arm around my shoulders, and we slowly ambled our way back toward my car.

"I think we need to search Molly's room," I said. "That girl was clearly keeping secrets."

"Joan Lewis isn't going to like that." Galloway grimaced. "She's been on the phone constantly, wanting progress updates, she isn't going to appreciate us poking around in her home."

"I wonder what secret was so big that Molly would prefer her mom think she was dating Nick—a man her mother clearly disapproved of—over the truth?" I said. Then it hit me. "Dean Ackerman!"

"Who's Dean Ackerman?"

"He's a registered nurse at the Firefly Bay Residential Aged Care Facility," I said. "He's one of Molly's bosses. And he's been having an affair with Molly's best friend, Angela."

"You have been busy." Galloway gave me a squeeze. "You're thinking this Ackerman guy was having an affair with Molly, too? That's why she was okay with people thinking she was dating Nick?"

"It's a possibility." And definitely a reason why Molly would lie to her mom.

"Great work on Nick's alibi," Galloway said, matching his longer stride to my shorter one. "How did you crack that?"

"Oh, it was Seb!"

"Seb?"

"He brought back my coffee cup this morning and happened to see the murder board and a photo of Nick, who he recognized."

"Seb frequents a gay bar?"

I nodded. "Yes. Because he's gay."

Galloway's lips turned down as he shook his head. "Man, I didn't pick that up."

"Right? Me either! But anyway, yes, it turns out Seb is gay. He recognized Nick, gave us the name of the club, and Ben checked the CCTV footage. Nick was definitely there the night Molly died. But of course, you'll need to go the official route and get a warrant for the footage, etc."

Galloway chuckled. "Of course."

"Oh. Sidenote. Seb wants to know if we'd like to join him as chaperones at the school's junior dance tomorrow night."

"Chaperone a grade school dance? I'll pass."

"What? You don't like kids?"

"I love kids. But I can think of better things you and I could be doing with our free time than chaperoning a bunch of kids. Anyway, isn't that Seb's job, not ours?"

"You know, for all his extravertadness and bravado, I think he's just looking for a friendly face. I mean, they have him chaperoning this thing when he hasn't officially started school yet. He hasn't even met these kids."

"Well, that's something he should be taking up with the school," Galloway pointed out.

"Fair point." We'd reached my car, and I pivoted, linking my arms around Galloway's neck and stretching up on my toes to plant a kiss on him. "You left early this morning."

He returned my kiss with enthusiasm. "Mmmm," he said against my lips. "You were dead to the world. After your rough night, I thought I'd let you sleep in."

"Big of you." I grinned.

"I thought so," he agreed, and we laughed. Then I heard them. The word *angel* blew on the wind, wrapping around me and sending shivers down my spine.

"What's wrong?" Galloway held me away from him, peering into my face with concern.

I shook my head. "It's fine. Just my twelve ghosts have caught up. I wish I knew what they wanted. I wish I knew why they keep saying angel."

"They're still not talking?"

"Nuh-uh." I sighed. "I've had no luck finding out anything about them. Ben checked the records at the old folks' home. Nothing matches."

"Have you tried the hospital?"

"That's not a bad idea, I guess. I'll ask Ben to swing by and see if there are any recent deaths that match our ghosts. It's just... twelve deaths. Twelve elderly deaths. Screams retirement home, right?"

"What about some sort of seniors' vacation or tour or something?" Galloway suggested, and I stared at him, mouth agape. Why hadn't I thought of that?

"You're a genius!" I kissed him again, then opened my car door. "Gotta run. If I can stay a step ahead of them, I might actually make some headway on my cases."

"Cases? As in, plural?"

"Yeah. Molly," I held up one finger, "and the twelve ghosts." I held up a second finger.

"Drive safe." Galloway smiled and waved, standing on the footpath watching as I pulled out and left him in the rear-view just as the twelve ghosts appeared at the end of Nick's street.

"Okay, okay, think," I said to myself as I sped away. "Nick is off the hook. He couldn't have killed Molly. Yet Molly lied to her mom about meeting Nick that night. So, who was she meeting? A secret lover? A lover that wasn't going to be secret for much longer since Molly had told Sharon she intended to break up with Nick. Or was that another lie? And surely, if that had been Molly's intention, she'd have talked with Nick about it since theirs wasn't a real relationship? What were you up to, Molly Lewis?

The *Ghostbusters* theme song blared from my phone. I answered the call via the car's Bluetooth.

"Audrey, love, it's Mom."

"Hey, Mom. What's up?"

"Just reminding you that it's Dad's birthday tomorrow. Family dinner at our place."

"I hadn't forgotten," I lied through my teeth. "We're not going to Delgorno's for dinner?" Every year, we celebrated Dad's birthday at his favorite Italian restaurant.

"Sort of. We're ordering takeout from Delgorno's. They deliver now. It's just easier with all the grandkids if we have it here."

"Sure." I got that. My sister had a toddler and a baby, Isabelle and baby Grace. My brother had two toddlers, Madeline and Nathaniel. We were at that stage where family get-togethers were chaotic, especially with Madeline in the sweet spot between two and four—that magical age where the terrible twos stretch on for a decade. As much as I loved the little munchkin, her tantrums were epic. Convincing her to sit quietly at a family dinner? Impossible.

"Do you need me to bring anything?" I asked dutifully, knowing she'd say no.

"Just Kade." I could hear the smile in Mom's voice.

"Done."

"See you tomorrow night. Around six."

"See ya, Mom." I disconnected the call and headed toward Sugar Maple Lane. It was a bit of a running joke that I bought Dad the same birthday gift every year, but heck, it was what he wanted, and I was happy to oblige—especially as he was one of those men who, when asked, said he didn't want anything. So, every year, I bought him a hundred-dollar bottle of single malt Scotch whisky. It worked for both of us.

Pulling up outside the liquor store, I hurried inside, almost running down Angela Brady in the process.

"Watch it!" She staggered sideways as our shoulders connected, and I ricocheted in the opposite direction with a breathless, "Sorry!"

I managed to right myself seconds before colliding with an impressive wine display.

"Oh, hey, Angela," I said once I recognized who I'd bumped into. "Fancy seeing you here."

She peered at me as if trying to place who I was.

"Audrey Fitzgerald, private investigator," I prompted.

Recognition dawned.

"Oh, right, yeah, yeah." She nodded and tightened her grip on the brown paper bag she held. "It's been a day."

"I bet." It wasn't even lunchtime yet, and here she was stocking up on liquor. But then she had just dumped her married lover, and her best friend had died. I couldn't exactly blame her, although looking at her now, she wasn't the wreck I'd have been if I were in her shoes. No, Angela Brady was immaculately groomed, not a hair out of place. Clean jeans, a crisp button-down, and a smart linen jacket completed the look. She could have stepped out of a fashion magazine.

"Actually, I'm glad I ran into you," I said. "I have a question."

"Oh?" She glanced around, keen to be gone.

"Is it possible Dean was having other... affairs?"

Her mouth turned down, and she shrugged. "That's a question you'll have to ask him."

"Oh, I intend to. I just wondered if maybe Molly had said anything?"

Angela snorted. "Molly and Dean? Highly doubtful. She didn't like him. She was constantly warning me to stay away from him."

"But wasn't that because he was married?"

"That, amongst other things."

"What other things?"

"She just said he couldn't be trusted."

"Did you agree with her assessment?"

"Well, clearly, he's a cheat." She sniffed. "And he's probably an addict."

My brows shot up. "An addict? Like, a drug addict?"

She huffed out a breath. "Look, you really need to go and talk to him about this. All I know is that pretty much every time I've been with him, he's popped a pill."

"Ohhh, you mean a blue pill? For...you know?" I raised one finger in a salute.

Angela laughed. "No, not Viagra. He has a bad back. He's constantly taking painkillers. Look, I gotta go. I've got a date to get ready for."

"A date? You only broke up with Dean this morning!" I blinked in surprise.

Another heavy sigh. "Dean was a bit of fun. Then he got boring. I was not invested in our *relationship,* if you could even call it that. So, yes, I ended it. Like I said to Dean this morning, despite what he may hope, I don't intend to sit at home moping over him."

"You weren't in love."

She laughed. "Far from it. Dean was a means to an end. An itch that needed scratching. He had fantasies that he'd leave his wife and we'd be together forever, but that was never going to happen." Before I could ask any more questions, she spun on her heel and walked out.

"That was close." Reece, an employee of the Burning Kite liquor store, grinned from behind the counter. "Thought you were going to topple another display."

I sniffed. "That only happened once."

"Twice," he corrected.

"It's rude to keep count," I said, ambling over to the counter.

"What can I get you today, Audrey?" he asked.

"It's Dad's birthday tomorrow."

"Ah." Reece nodded. "Ten-year-old single malt Scotch whisky?"

I was touched that he remembered. "You got it."

While Reece rang up my purchase, I pondered my conversation with Angela. She said it herself. She wasn't invested in her relationship with Dean, which meant she had no motive for wanting her friend Molly dead. But that didn't mean Molly and Dean hadn't been in a relationship as well. It just meant that Angela either didn't know or didn't care. But given how Molly felt about Dean, he would be an odd choice.

"I'm really going to have to talk with Dean," I said.

"Dean who?" Reece asked, passing me the bottle of whisky in a brown paper bag with a flaming red kite emblazoned on it.

"Oh, sorry, talking to myself," I apologized with a smile. "Thanks, Reece. Have a nice day."

"You too, Audrey. Try not to bump into anyone else."

I laughed and waved as I headed out of the store and back to my car just as twelve ghosts rounded the corner. Were they getting faster? But I had an idea. The ghosts hadn't followed me to the Firefly Bay Residential Aged Care facility. And since Dean worked there, now was a good time to go and have a word with the local Lothario. Sans ghosts.

Chapter Ten

I'd remembered on the way to the aged care facility that Dean was on nights, so, therefore, wouldn't be at work at lunchtime on Saturday, so I about-faced and headed home. I'd just have to put up with my ghost situation and push through. I was back at my desk, on my computer, trying to find more links to Molly and who would want to kill her. Of course, that list was pretty short. Nick had alibied out. Angela had no motive. Dean was my number one suspect. I was currently running his name through one of my PI databases, searching for his address and anything else that may be of interest.

"What about Dean's wife?" Ben suggested, leaning over my shoulder.

I leaned back in my chair, stroking my chin. "You know, that's not a bad idea. Let's just say that Molly and Dean are having a little tryst, and Dean's wife finds out about it? There's motive right there."

"You do realize you're basing that motive on non-facts. We don't know Molly and Dean were even an item."

"True." I yawned. "And Angela told me Molly couldn't stand Dean."

"That could have been a smoke screen to throw Angela off the scent."

"But what I know of Molly, she seemed like a really nice girl. Not the type, I would have thought, to have an affair with her best friend's boyfriend. Who also happens to be married," I added. Molly just didn't strike me as that type of person. "I really wish her ghost were here."

"You've got these guys." Ben jerked his thumb toward the twelve ghosts crammed in behind us. They were blissfully silent—for now. I just prayed they stayed that way. And I prayed I could find out their story and help them move on before dinner at my parents' house tomorrow night.

"That reminds me," I said to Ben, "Galloway had a good idea."

"About?"

"These guys. A seniors' tour or cruise of some sort. They were all on a tour, and the bus crashed, killing them all. That would explain twelve deaths at the same time."

"That would've reached the news, surely," Ben said.

"Angel!" the ghosts practically yelled, scaring the bejesus out of me.

"Aargh!" I yelled back, hand on my thundering heart. "Will you guys stop that! I'm not going to be able to help you if I die from a heart attack!"

In a fit of pique, I shot out of my chair and stomped to the kitchen. "There is not enough coffee in the world to deal with that lot," I grumbled under my breath, shoving a cup under the coffee machine and jabbing at the button.

"Fitz?" Ben approached with an air of caution. "Not like you to lose your temper like that."

I hung my head. "I know. I'm sorry. I just…" I lifted my arms and let them flop to my sides again. "I'm frustrated. I don't know how to help them."

"It's okay. We'll work it out. We always do." He stepped forward and wrapped me in an icy cold ghost hug, and I let him. The coolness was soothing, and I closed my eyes, wishing for the briefest moment that he was here with me again. Alive.

"Hey." He stepped back and peered into my face. "Are those tears?"

I blinked rapidly. "No." My vision blurred, and I turned my attention back to the coffee machine. This is what sleep deprivation did to you. Made you all emotional and stuff.

"Tell you what, I'll check out all the news stations and see what I can do to track down the identities of these ghosts," Ben said from behind me. "You focus on Molly."

"Okay." It would be so much easier if the twelve ghosts would at least speak with us and tell us their names.

"Fitz? Stop worrying. Have your coffee, then go talk to Dean and or his wife."

I pulled myself together and spun to face him with a smile on my face. "You're right."

"I'm always right."

"Not always."

"Name a time when I wasn't." He crossed his arms over his chest and raised a brow.

"Oh, I can name several." I matched his pose, scouring my brain for one example and coming up empty. Then a memory sparked, and I snapped my fingers. "You were sixteen and convinced Mindy Whittaker was in love with you!" I pointed at him triumphantly.

He blinked. "You remember that?" I didn't miss the wash of color that crept across his cheekbones. Who knew ghosts could blush?

I barked out a laugh. "She was your teacher, and you had a crush. I'll never forget that."

Ben shook his head. "This is what happens with growing up and staying friends with your neighbors," he grumbled.

"There's not a lot I don't know about you, Ben Delaney," I chortled.

"Just remember that I can say the same about you, Audrey Fitzgerald," he teased back. He was right, of course. We'd grown up next door to each other, and we'd remained friends from childhood into adulthood. I knew all of Ben's secrets, but unfortunately, he knew all of mine. The good, the bad, and the ugly. Not to mention the embarrassing, and with my clumsy gene, there were tons of those.

"Yes, but you're a ghost. Who you gonna tell?" I shot back.

"Dang! Good point." Then we burst into laughter. I laughed so hard my ribs ached, and I may have peed a little. It felt good. The laughing part, not the pee part.

"I had a thought," I giggled, wiping the tears of laughter from under my eyes. "What if Dean's wife mistook Molly for Angela?"

Ben stopped laughing and looked at me, his face morphing from joyful to severe. "You know, that's plausible," he said.

I sobered. "Right? Providing that she— what's her name? Katherine?—doesn't know Dean's work colleagues, that is."

"Go tidy yourself up and get over there," Ben ordered.

"Coffee first."

"Fine." He sighed with theatrical flare. "Coffee first."

* * *

Dean and Katherine Ackerman lived in an ordinary house in a typical suburb. As I pulled up out front, I sat for a minute and scanned the row of almost identical houses.

"What are you thinking?" Ben asked from the passenger seat. He'd decided to join me at the last minute, and I didn't have the energy to argue. My twelve ghosts weren't going anywhere...except to follow me around at a snail's pace. If I timed it right, I could get in, speak to either of the Ackermans, and get out before they turned up.

"Oh, just how...bland all the houses look. No. Not bland. Just... the same. I'd probably wander into the wrong house constantly if I lived here."

"Affordable housing," Ben said, following my gaze.

"Right, let's do this." I opened the car door and slid out. "You'll go inside and do a recon?"

"Absolutely." Ben walked with me to the Ackermans' front door, but he walked right on through while I stopped to knock. I stood on the porch, waiting. And waiting. I knocked again, louder. Dean was on night shift which meant he should be home now, probably sleeping, but I didn't have any qualms about waking him. Not if he—or his wife—was Molly's killer.

"You can stop knocking. No one's home." Ben stepped through the front door, forcing me to take a rapid step backward. Big mistake. I stepped right off the porch and landed on my rear on the grass.

"Ouch." I cursed, clambering to my feet and rubbing my stinging rump.

"Sorry! Are you okay?"

"Just another bruise to add to the collection." It was my go-to joke whenever I took a tumble.

"Your clumsiness gets worse when you're tired," Ben said.

"I know." I yawned. "Maybe I'll take a nap and then come back here later, try the Ackermans again. I wonder where they are?"

"Katherine is probably at work," Ben said. "But I was expecting to find Dean asleep. You said he was on night shift, along with Angela."

"Correct. That's what the schedule says." It was what I'd been expecting too.

"I wonder if he's with Angela?"

I frowned. "I doubt it. I witnessed them breaking up. And it wasn't a show for my benefit. They didn't know I was coming," I quickly added when Ben opened his mouth to interrupt.

"Another girlfriend, perhaps?" Ben suggested.

"Where does he find the energy?" I yawned again and blinked. My eyes were starting to feel like I'd bathed them in sand.

"Come on, let's get you home for that nap. You're asleep on your feet."

"Best idea you've had all day." I'd just pulled away from the curb when my phone rang, and Galloway's name flashed on the screen.

I punched the answer call button on my steering wheel. "Hey," I greeted him.

"Hey," he responded, and then I heard a ruckus in the background.

"Where are you? What's going on?" I could hear a woman yelling but couldn't make out the words.

"Hang on a sec. I'll move outside." I waited, could hear Galloway's footsteps and other various muffled sounds as he moved away from the yelling woman. "Sorry about that," he said.

"Who was that?"

"Joan Lewis."

"Man, she isn't happy." I knew I was pointing out the obvious but couldn't help myself. "What's happened? Is there a break in the case?"

"No, nothing like that. Remember we were talking this morning about Molly having secrets?"

"Yep."

"Well, I figured I'd save some time and ask Joan if she'd let us search Molly's room."

"Without a warrant?"

"Yeah. I mean, I can get one. Molly is a murder victim. But I figured Joan wants the killer caught and she'd agree to let us search without a warrant."

"I take it that didn't go down well?"

"She's demanding we get a warrant."

"Okay." I shrugged my shoulders. Joan was well within her rights to request that. I was surprised she wouldn't let the police in, but that was her prerogative. "So, you're calling me because?"

"She said you—and only you—can come in and search Molly's room."

"But I'm not police."

"Exactly."

I chewed my lip. "If I do this...if I search Molly's room and find something, would that be considered hindering a police investigation?"

"Very good, Fitz." Ben was nodding like a bobblehead beside me.

"Only if you don't tell us what you found," Galloway replied.

"And hand it over, I assume?"

"Correct."

I hesitated, thinking about what to do next. Galloway was basically asking that I do the search on behalf of the police. While I could definitely do that, I also had a duty to my client.

"Here's what I think you should do," Ben said, reading my mind. "Head to Joan's now. But the police can't be there—get Galloway and his team to leave. Having them camp out on the front lawn while they wait for a warrant is only going to inflame the situation. That gives you some breathing space if you find anything."

"Hang on," I said to Galloway, then whispered to Ben, "You think I'm going to find something?"

"Don't you?"

"I guess. So, whatever I find, I can take a copy or a photograph or whatever *before* I give it to the police?"

Ben was nodding again. "Right."

I raised my voice, so Galloway could hear. "Okay, fine, I'm on my way. Tell Joan that I'm coming, but you all have to clear out. She sounded pretty hysterical."

"We're leaving," Galloway assured me. "It'll take a while to get a judge to sign a warrant on the weekend anyway. I'll let Joan know you're on the way. That should calm her down."

"So, I guess I'll need to come to the station after? To report what I find, if anything."

"That'd be great."

We said our farewells and hung up. I liked that Galloway hadn't put a timeframe on when I had to report in because if I did find something in Molly's room, you could bet your patootie I was going to investigate it first. A fact Galloway no doubt already knew, maybe even counted on.

Joan Lewis's house was a two-story building, a cute cottage-type affair. "Nice place," I said out of the corner of my mouth as Ben and I walked up the garden path. There was not a police car in sight. Birds were chirping in the trees, bees were buzzing, you wouldn't think Joan had been screaming her lungs out a short while ago. I rang the bell and stood back to wait.

"Oh, thank God you're here!" Joan flung the door open and ushered me inside, sticking her head out after I'd walked past her to check that the police had left. "The cops were here. They wanted to search Molly's room!"

"Yeah, I got a call," I said. "Is it okay if *I* take a look in Molly's room?"

Joan, her eyes bloodshot, her nose red, nodded. "Yes. You can. I trust you."

"You don't trust the police?" I fished around in my bag for a pair of latex gloves and snapped them on.

"Do you? You were involved in that investigation last year, bringing down those corrupt cops."

Who could forget? Officer Ian Mills had made my life a living hell. I'd been glad to see the back of him.

"That investigation was pretty extensive," I told her. "I don't think we have any bad cops now."

She sniffed and tilted her head back, nose in the air. "I'd prefer not to take any chances. Here, Molly's room is this way." She led me upstairs; Molly's was the first door on the right.

"I'll leave you to it." Joan hesitated in the doorway, clearly reluctant to step foot inside. "I haven't touched anything. It hurts to be in here." Her eyes swam, and a tear overflowed to trickle down her cheek.

"How about you go make us a coffee, and I'll be down as soon as I'm finished? I'll try and be quick."

Ben was already at work, Molly's laptop sat on the desk under the window, and he had his hand buried in it, digging through the electronic device. After Joan had departed, I started with the bed, lifting the mattress, checking under the pillow, and slowly making my way around the room. It took longer than expected, and I was starting to think we weren't going to find anything of importance when Ben shouted, "I've found something!"

"What?" I hurried over to where he was standing in the middle of the desk. "The laptop?" He'd spent the entire time with the computer, digging through Molly's digital life.

"No, no. Under the desk. There's something taped to the underside of the desk."

Pulling out the chair, I dropped to my hands and knees and peered at the underside of the desk. Sure enough, a small rectangular object was taped to the wood. Pulling it free, I crawled out and held it up. "A USB."

"Let me see." Ben went to take it from me but couldn't. Instead, I held it aloft between my forefinger and thumb, and Ben touched it with his own finger.

"Anything?" I asked.

"A bunch of data. Numbers. It's not making sense to me."

I shoved the USB into my pocket. "I'll make a copy of it and then give it to Galloway."

Chapter Eleven

Dragging myself through the front door, I headed to the living room and collapsed on the sofa. It was nap time. There was no more avoiding it. I didn't even have the energy to heave myself upstairs to bed; the couch would do, and copying the USB would have to wait.

Positioning a cushion beneath my head, I closed my eyes and drifted off to blissful, restful sleep. I'm not sure how long I was out. It could have been minutes, or it could have been hours, but something dragged me from my peaceful slumber. Something quite horrifyingly rank. My nose twitched. My nostrils burned. My eyes watered. What in the heck was that stench?

Cracking open my eyes, I squinted at the ceiling as if the answer could be found there. Of course, the ceiling was fine, as you'd expect it to be. The stench was emanating from one gray ball of fluff currently curled up against my side.

"Thor?" I gagged. Now I'd opened my mouth, I could taste it. I could taste a smell; it was that bad. "Is that you?"

Thor slowly opened one eye. "Hmmm?" he asked, voice drowsy.

"That smell." I wheezed, gasping for breath, eyes burning. "Is it you? Have you rolled in something?"

"No." He sat up and yawned. I leaned forward and sniffed his fur. Nope. No smell of roadkill on him, not directly, but still, a hideous gas hung in the air, clogging my lungs. It crashed into my nose and nestled in my nostrils like a pungent, wet cotton ball, smelling disturbingly like a mouthful of hair and an old, unwanted sponge. Only worse. Much, much worse. This stuff could strip the paint off the walls, yet despite that, I was unable to move, unable to drag myself out of the haze of misery that had me pinned to the couch.

I lay there, puzzling over it while I watched Thor. I watched his eyes narrow, his tail flick, then an unmistakable *toot* reached my ears.

"You farted!" I accused.

"Well, you started it," he shot back, rubbing his whiskers in my direction. "If you hadn't snored...."

"I don't snore!"

"Yes, you do." He ignored my indignant huff. "It's a very disturbing snore, by the way. I don't think anyone could sleep with that racket going on."

"Oh, so I'm not allowed a peaceful sleep? And I suppose you were sleeping just fine? It's a shame I woke you," I said with as much self-righteousness as I could muster.

Thor might have had all the charm of an overgrown chickpea, but there was something so adorable about him, I just couldn't stay mad. But I was concerned. "What—exactly—have you been eating?" It was clearly not from his approved diet list, which was mercifully short. Diet kibble. Diet wet food. Vet-approved food that did not induce peeling paint from the walls, soul-destroying, farts.

"We had snacks from next door!" Bandit piped up. I hadn't noticed her curled up on the armchair. I sat bolt upright, turning to her.

"Didn't I tell you not to go next door begging for food?" And hadn't I warned Seb of that exact thing? Do not feed the animals! I mean, honestly, how hard is it to follow simple instructions?

"He offered." Thor sniffed. "I'm not going to say no."

"What did he give you?"

"Fish sticks!" Bandit said with glee. "They were yummy."

I narrowed my eyes. They may have been yummy going down, but the smells coming from Thor's rear end were far from delightful. "Are you farting too?" I asked Bandit.

"What's a fart?" she asked.

"Passing gas from your butt," Thor told her.

"Ohhh, those funny noises your tummy makes before you poop?"

Oh, good grief. I swung my legs to the floor and pointed to the back door. "Outside. Both of you. Do not come back until you have no more gas left to pass." I watched the pair of them trot across the floor and out the cat door while I was left to suffer in the dank fumes they'd left behind.

"There's not enough air freshener in the world to get rid of this smell."

"Angel!" my twelve ghosts agreed. A glance at my phone told me I'd been asleep for twenty minutes, and despite the napalm hanging in the air, I was surprisingly refreshed. Opening all the windows to air out the living room, I made myself a coffee, then settled into my office chair, USB plugged into the computer.

Ben was right. A bunch of data. It was some sort of text document, but nothing like I'd seen before. My twelve ghosts hovered behind me, and it was almost as if they were watching over my shoulder, but each time I glanced around, their eyes were focused straight ahead. I turned in my chair to face them. They didn't react. So, I sat and waited. Didn't have to wait long. The woman directly in front of me cast her eyes my way before quickly redirecting her gaze.

"Ah-ha!" I pointed at her triumphantly. "Caught you! Come on, y'all can stop pretending and relax. I know you're watching me."

En masse, their rigid figures relaxed, their shoulders rounded and slumped forward. If they were corporeal, I imagined I'd hear bones cracking and popping.

"So," I continued, "you were pretending you weren't interested in this." I turned in my chair and tapped my monitor. "Why?"

"Angel," the woman in front said. She was short, plump, with a head full of curly white hair.

"Is that all you can say? Angel?"

"Angel," she repeated with a nod.

"Well, that's frustrating."

"Angel," she agreed. But it was a breakthrough. They'd never been this interactive before. Was it the power of Thor's farts that had brought about this phenomenon? Or was I somehow closer to discovering what had happened to them? Which was ironic considering I'd been working on Molly's case, not theirs.

"Wait!" I swung around again. "Are your deaths in any way connected to Molly Lewis?"

"Angel," the apparent spokes-ghost said. No nod or shake of the head, merely a shrug of the shoulders.

"So, that's a firm maybe?"

"Angel."

"Were you all residents of the Firefly Bay Aged Care Facility?" It was a long shot. I'd assumed they'd all died at the same time, but what if they hadn't?

"Angel," they all replied in unison, backed up with a firm nod of heads.

"Now we're getting somewhere." My heart skipped a beat as adrenaline surged through me. It could not be a coincidence that Molly was a nurse at the home, and the twelve elderly ghosts currently haunting me had all been past residents.

"Ben!" I called. I hadn't seen him since I woke up from my nap. Knowing I don't like him watching me sleep, he'd most likely gone visiting around the neighborhood to see who happened to have the shopping channel blaring from their television.

"You called?" He appeared in the doorway, shot a look at my ghost posse, then back at me. "What's this then? Have we had a breakthrough?"

"We have." I brought him up to speed on my theory that the twelve ghosts were linked to the aged care home. And Molly. "And they seem awfully interested in this." I tapped the monitor with the data Molly had gathered on display. "I've yet to make sense of it. These guys probably know what it is, but all they can say is Angel. I think if I approach it in terms of hot and cold, we might get somewhere."

"Worth a try," Ben agreed.

"Right. Let's go over what we know. The last death at the facility was Cecilia Fairweather. Died in her sleep. Are any of you Cecilia?" I'd asked them before, but they'd been unresponsive. But today, for a reason I had yet to understand, I was able to communicate with my twelve ghosts. Progress at last.

A tall, thin woman with short, white hair raised her hand.

"Holy crap-a-doodle." I gasped. "You're Cecilia?"

She nodded. "Angel."

"Excellent." I grabbed a blank USB from the top drawer and copied Molly's data. "I'm going to drop this off to Galloway, then go visit the home, find out what I can about Cecilia's death."

"You think there's something suspicious about it?" Ben asked.

"Don't you? Her ghost is standing right here with eleven of her friends. If she'd passed peacefully in her sleep, then why didn't she cross over? Why is she here? And now that I know they weren't all victims of a bus rollover, that they actually died at different times, I can dig through the records—or rather, you can—and maybe we can identify all of them."

"And Molly?"

"I'm going to call into Dean's on the way," I told him. Molly's case was my first priority, but it would be nice to get to the bottom of my ghostly situation and send these guys on their way. I couldn't imagine it was fun for them either, being stuck here.

Ten minutes later, I was pulling into the parking lot at the police department. Sitting in the car, I couldn't help but notice my fingers were clenched around the wheel, and my anxiety levels were spiking. No surprises. Despite everything, I still have a visceral reaction every time I see a police vehicle, and there were two currently occupying space in the parking lot. Galloway's secret task force to rid the department of corrupt cops had done the job. Yet, Ben had been collateral damage, and there was nothing anyone could do about it. I'd been by his side when he'd been forced out of the job he loved by a bent system, and my bias against the police had been a difficult hurdle to overcome. Of course, it was helped along greatly by dating a smoking hot detective.

Prying my fingers from the wheel, I dragged a deep breath into my lungs and slowly expelled it before climbing out of the car.

Pushing through the station doors, I waved to Officer Sarah Jacobs, who'd glanced up when I entered.

"Oh, hey, Audrey." She smiled. "Here to see Galloway? He's in his office; go on through."

"Thanks." Heading down the corridor, I came to Galloway's door and stood leaning against the frame, watching as Galloway pecked at his keyboard with two fingers, face intent as he worked.

"Hey," I eventually said when he failed to notice me standing there ogling him.

His eyes shot to mine, a flicker of surprise quickly replaced by a warmth that heated to a sizzle. Galloway was a combination of cop and cowboy, and as I drank in his dark good looks, he flashed that sexy dimple of his, and my knees just about gave out. I snagged the chair opposite his desk before I made a fool of myself.

"Hey you." He grinned. "How's it going?"

"Oh, it's going good." I grinned back. How could it be I'd been dating this man for over a year, and he still had the ability to reduce me to a pile of mush just by saying hey and smiling at me? You'd think I'd have built up some sort of immunity by now, but alas...

"Earth to Audrey." He laughed, and I realized I'd missed what he'd said because I was busy fantasizing about him. Again.

"Sorry." I cleared my throat, feeling my cheeks heat.

"I love that about you." Galloway's expression softened, and he leaned back in his chair, his eyes all over me.

"Oh, yeah? What's that?" I fanned my face. Was it getting hot in here, or was it just me?

"That you blush." He flashed that dimple again, and it distracted me so that I almost missed what he said again. Then the penny dropped.

"Wash your mouth out. I do not." I felt myself blush even harder, and he barked out a laugh.

"Do you have something for me?" he asked.

"Do I ever," I drawled, and he laughed even harder.

"Work-related, Audrey. Did you search Molly's room?"

"Oh. Right." My face was practically on fire. Was thirty too early for menopause? Digging into my bag, I pulled out the USB and held it up. "Found this taped to the underside of her desk."

Galloway leaned forward and took the flash drive from me, the brush of his fingers against mine sending a spark of heat through me. "Great work," he said, then he was plugging in the USB, and his eyes were on the file, ignoring me.

"You're welcome." Knowing he would be one hundred percent engrossed in what was on the USB, I stood and headed to the door. "Oh, yeah, before I forget, are you free for dinner tomorrow night? It's Dad's birthday." I glanced over my shoulder, but he didn't look up.

"Yeah, yeah, your mom already called," he said absently.

"She did?"

"Mmmm." He finally raised his head and looked at me. "Isn't that school dance with your new best friend, Seb, tomorrow night?" he reminded me.

"Oh, shoot, you're right. No biggie, I haven't given Seb an answer yet anyway. I'll just tell him we can't go."

"I wasn't planning on it anyway." Galloway's eyes were back on his computer.

"Right. Well, I'll see ya later. Will you let me know if you work out what all those numbers mean?"

"Sure."

I left, smiling to myself. One thing Galloway and I had in common was that we liked a good puzzle, and Molly's death was definitely that.

Chapter Twelve

Dean Ackerman was not at home, but his wife was. Katherine stood in the open doorway in her Lululemon active gear, platinum blonde hair pulled into a ponytail with tendrils escaping to curl softly around her perfectly made-up face.

"Yes?"

"Is Dean in?" I asked.

She eyed me up and down. "Who's asking?"

Pulling a business card from my bag, I held it out to her. "Audrey Fitzgerald, Delaney Investigations," I said. "I'm looking into the death of Molly Lewis."

"Oh, yes, I heard. How terribly sad. But what does it have to do with my husband?"

"I believe he worked with Molly?"

Katherine slapped her forehead. "Yes! Of course." She stood back and gestured for me to come inside. I stepped over the threshold, directly into their living room. My eyes quickly scanned over the oversized beige sofa with colorful throw pillows, a chunky wooden coffee table, and a massive television in one corner. It was a homey room. Warm, welcoming, comfortable. In the background, I could faintly hear music playing. *Black Magic* by Little Mix. *Coincidence?* I think not.

"Can I get you a coffee?" she offered.

"No, I'm good." Words I never thought would leave my mouth. But I was on a time crunch, so no time to sit around enjoying a coffee when there was a killer to catch. I ignored the fact that I frequently accepted offers of coffee from suspects. "So? Is Dean home?" I prompted.

"Oh, no. Sorry. He's at work."

"At work? I thought he was on nights?"

"He picked up an extra shift. I guess they're short-staffed, you know, because of Molly."

"Right," I nodded. "Wow. An extra shift after working all night. That's gotta be tiring."

"I'm more worried about what it does to his back." Katherine sighed, popping one hip and resting her hand on it, her manicured nails tapping. "They work him too hard there. It's really not good for him."

"Oh?"

"Too bad his injury didn't happen at work, then we'd at least get worker's comp, but he slipped on our driveway." She pointed out the window, and I automatically glanced outside.

"Sorry to hear that. Was he badly hurt?"

"A slipped disc. He was in so much pain. Still is."

"Oh, so this was recent? Should he even be working?"

She waved a hand around in a vague gesture. "It happened last year. Doctors say he should be well and truly healed by now, that normally," she air quoted, "it takes six weeks for an injury like his to heal. But Dean still has pain. He's had all the scans and x-rays, and doctors still can't tell us why. Our insurance won't cover any more tests."

"That has to put a strain on your marriage," I prompted. Seems Dean's bad back didn't stop him from fooling around, which made him a dog in my book. But it appeared Katherine wasn't aware of her husband's philandering ways, and it wasn't my job to tell her. Tempting though. Maybe I'd let it slip once the case was closed if it didn't all come out in the meantime. Especially if it turned out that Dean killed Molly. Katherine would find out the truth about her husband, one way or another.

She smiled, her face softening. "Don't get me wrong, he's a good man. He regularly brings me a cup of tea in bed before he heads out for his night shift."

I had to bite my tongue about the good man comment.

"You don't mind being here alone? When he's on nights?"

"Actually," she leaned forward conspiratorially, "I sleep so much better when he's not here. I think it's having the bed to myself, you know? But don't tell him I said that." She giggled.

I smiled, tight-lipped. "Your secret is safe with me," I told her. "I should go. I'm on my way to the Firefly Bay Residential Aged Care facility now, so I'll catch him there."

"Okay." Katherine smiled and ushered me to the door.

"Out of interest, were you home, alone, the night Molly died?" I asked as I stepped onto the front porch.

"Oh yes. Dean brought me a cup of tea while I was catching up on my favorite soap, but then I got so sleepy I couldn't keep my eyes open, so I went to bed. Slept like a baby all night long. Why? Do I need an alibi?" She blinked her long fake eyelashes.

"Just crossing all the t's and dotting the i's," I assured her.

"Well, tell my babycakes I said hi." She wiggled her fingers in a wave and closed the door.

"Thoughts?" I asked Ben as we headed back to the car. He'd disappeared into the rest of the house while I'd been speaking with Katherine and had only just rejoined me.

"I think she's clueless about her husband cheating," Ben said. "She keeps a lovely home, spends way too much on fashion, especially considering she works part-time as a beautician—that can't pull in much cash, she only works about ten hours a week."

"How do you know that?"

"She has a schedule pinned to the fridge and a payslip on the kitchen bench."

"Hmm. Maybe that's why Dean pulls extra shifts? If that's even true. Maybe he's lying about the shifts to his wife because he's out sleeping with other women."

"Could be," Ben agreed.

"So, he's got this gorgeous wife who takes good care of herself and their home, yet he's risking losing her by playing away. Why do that?"

"Maybe their sex life isn't... you know... happening."

"She did say he has a bad back," I said, sliding behind the steering wheel. "Maybe that killed things off in the bedroom. But it doesn't make sense. His back obviously isn't stopping him from sleeping with other women. And if it was an issue in his marriage, I'm pretty sure Katherine would have accidentally divulged that. She seemed pretty open to me."

"I did find a lot of painkillers in the bathroom cabinet," Ben said. "Like, a lot."

"Which makes sense if he has a bad back. Anything else?"

"No Viagra if that's what you're thinking," Ben teased.

I laughed. "I wasn't, but ewww, thanks for putting that thought in my head."

"There were some women's multi-purpose vitamins and a prescription bottle with Katherine's name on it."

"Right. I wonder what they're for?"

"Could be anything," Ben said. "She seems a little hyper to me."

"Hyper? Really? You got that from the whopping five minutes I spent talking with her standing in her living room?" I did not get the sense that Katherine Ackerman was hyper.

"No, I got it from the spare bedroom, which is full of what appears to be discarded hobbies. They range from craft pursuits like flower pressing to needlepoint to dressmaking, onto pottery, painting, and bird watching."

"Wow. Maybe you're right."

"Given she only works two half days a week, I'm guessing she has a lot of time to fill and a short attention span."

"I'm curious why she's working part-time," I admitted. "No kids. She appears healthy. Why not work full-time?"

"Is it pertinent? To the case?"

"Probably not." I sighed. "I'm just curious. I think I'd be bored if I didn't have work."

It was a short drive to the aged care facility, and Ben and I spent the time discussing what hobbies I'd pursue if I lived a life of leisure. Apparently, according to Ben, not many would be safe, considering how clumsy I am.

Pulling up in the parking lot of the aged care home, I left the engine running. "Before you go visit with your dad," I said, turning to face him where he hovered half in, half above the passenger seat, "could you have a go at their computer system and see if we can't find out who the other eleven ghosts are?"

"Of course." By the time I'd turned off the engine and opened the door, Ben was gone, leaving me to check in to the facility on my own. All visitors had to sign in and out, and as I was writing out my name, I caught sight of Sharon Mooney hurrying past. She saw me and faltered, then changed direction and headed over.

"Miss Fitzgerald," she said, a note of surprise in her voice. "I didn't expect to see you here again so soon."

"Call me Audrey, please," I replied. Sharon looked, well, exhausted, to put it politely. "Are you okay?" I asked in concern, reaching out to touch her arm.

She snatched her arm away and winced. "Darn bursitis," she muttered under her breath, rubbing at her shoulder, then, "I'm fine. It's been a little hectic."

"Right." I nodded. I could only imagine. "I'm actually here to speak with Dean Ackerman?"

"Dean?" Her eyebrows shot up.

"He is on duty, right? His wife said he'd picked up an extra shift?"

"Yes, yes, he's here somewhere." Her brow furrowed. "How's the investigation going?"

"It's still ongoing."

"Right. Well, I'll leave you to it. You might find Dean in the treatment room." She pointed, and I noticed a door down a corridor with a sign saying Treatment Room.

"Thanks." I headed toward the room in question. The door was closed, and when I turned the knob, locked as well. A single window opened into the corridor, and I cupped my hands to my face and pressed them to the glass, peering inside.

Inside was a treatment bed, a stainless steel trolley on wheels that had a collection of dressings lined up on the top, a long bench with cupboards beneath with labels I couldn't quite read. There were three oxygen bottles stacked in a corner and a tall stand-alone cabinet with a digital keypad lock. Dean Ackerman was standing in the middle of the room with his back to me. I tapped the glass, and he jumped, swiveling his neck to look at me over his shoulder.

With a frown, he came to the door and opened it.

"Yes?" he asked. "What do you want?"

"Do you always keep the treatment door locked?" I asked.

"Yes. The drugs cabinet is in here." He nodded toward the tall cabinet with the digital lock. "Plus, some residents like to wander, and they keep making off with the bandages," he added. "I repeat, what do you want?"

"Actually, I came to speak with you." I smiled brightly. "You might remember me? I was at Angela's this morning when she was dumping your ass?"

The color drained from his face, leaving him a lovely shade of gray.

"What?" he squeaked, perspiration dotting his forehead.

"Audrey Fitzgerald, Delaney Investigations," I continued, holding out a business card. He didn't take it, and I let my arm drop. "I've been hired to investigate the death of Molly Lewis."

He exhaled a pent-up breath. "Right. Nasty business, that."

"Indeed. So, where were you at the time of her death?"

"Here. Working. You can check."

"I intend to. And how long has the affair with Angela Brady been going on?" He started to sputter, but I held up a hand to stop him. "Please, don't try to deny it. I saw her breaking up with you with my own eyes, plus she's already confirmed it, so let's save some time by not lying."

He was shaking his head, his mouth downturned. "A couple of months maybe," he mumbled.

"I understand Molly found out about it and threatened to tell your wife."

"Yeah." He had the grace to look ashamed, his head bowed as he studied the tips of his shoes.

"And yet, you didn't break it off with Angela. She broke it off with you."

He sighed again. A big, heartfelt sigh. "Look, I don't expect you to understand, but I love my wife. I do. It's just that, at home, she can be... smothering. She gets bored at home by herself, so she's just in my ear constantly and all over me when I get home. It gets...irritating."

"So, why doesn't she work full-time? Get a pet? Find a hobby," that sticks, I added silently.

"Katherine has MS," Dean said. "Full-time work is out of the question. When she's tired, it triggers flare-ups. So, she has to take it easy."

"Oh, she didn't mention that." I blinked in shock. I'd had no idea Katherine was unwell.

"You talked to her?" He paled once more.

"Relax. I didn't out you. But you were telling me about you and Angela and Molly's ultimatum," I reminded him.

"Okay, fine. I intended to end it with Angela. She's a nice girl and all, but there's nothing romantic between us. It's just sex. I was hoping for a, how do you say, farewell performance? One last hoorah. But she wasn't up for it." He shrugged.

I wasn't sure I believed him. "Is there anyone else here that you're involved with? Past or present?"

His eyes darted away. "No."

"Liar."

He bit his lip, and a trickle of sweat made its way from his temple down to his ear. The silence grew, and I let it until the air was thick with unspoken words. I waited until he couldn't stand it any longer, and in all honesty, it wasn't much of a wait. Thirty seconds at best.

"Okay, fine. Janis Skinner. She works in the laundry room." He caved spectacularly.

"And this has been going on how long?"

"Since today," he admitted, and I couldn't contain the snort. "Really? So, straight from Angela dumping you into the arms of Janis. Wow. You don't waste any time."

"Just don't tell my wife," he pleaded.

I waggled my finger in his face. "No promises. You know, the police will be all up in your business as well, and let's just say they're not as discreet as me. Take my advice. Keep it in your pants and go on home to your wife. Your wife loves you very much. God only knows why." I pivoted on my heel, leaving him standing in the treatment room, his eyes boring into me. If Dean was the killer, then I'd just put a target on my back.

Chapter Thirteen

Raising my fist, I hammered on Seb's front door. Time to have it out with my neighbor who'd fed Thor and Bandit after I'd explicitly asked him not to. The door swung open, and he stood there, like an angel from heaven. I was surprised he wasn't bathed in some sort of holy light from above or at least had a halo.

"Hey, Audrey, how's things?" He smiled his mega-watt smile, and my irritation eased just a fraction. I was still mad. Just not *as* mad. Seb Castle had that effect on people.

"Did I, or did I not, ask you not to feed Bandit and Thor?" I asked, brushing past him. He'd finished unpacking, and Mrs. Hill's doily filled cottage was now a modern and sleek bachelor pad. "Nice," I added.

"Ah." He nodded, closing the front door behind me. "The fish sticks."

"Indeed." I crossed my arms over my chest and did my best to look angry. From the twitch of his lips, I suspected I looked more constipated than anything else. "May I also mention that those fish sticks gave Thor the worst gas? I mean, it's so bad I think I'm going to have to re-paint the walls and get new furniture."

"That bad?"

"Worse." I pouted.

"Audrey," Seb began, crossing to sling an arm around my shoulders and give me a squeeze. "I don't know how to tell you this, but your pets? They are terrors."

"Terrors? We are talking about the same critters here, right? Thor and Bandit?"

"The teddy bear cat, round." He mimed rubbing a round belly. "And the raccoon."

Definitely mine. I cocked my head. "What did they do?"

"Only the biggest heist in the history of heists!" Seb declared dramatically.

I narrowed my eyes, my mind racing. "Are we talking fish stick heists?"

Seb began pacing back and forth in his living room, his arms waving, face animated. "I had the back door propped open, carrying out the empty boxes into the back garden to flatten them down and put them in the recycling when there was this scratching coming from the front door. So, I opened the front door, and Bandit is there, chattering away to me with a great deal of excitement. So, I played along. I'm crouched in front of her, asking questions—as you do—when she just leaves. No goodbye. She just decided she was done. Only she took off at a run, which I thought was odd, but then I admit I don't know her that well and that could be normal behavior for Bandit." He paused to drag in a breath, then continued on before I could get a word in. "I closed the front door, and then I heard this noise from out back. I didn't think much of it, probably the wind, but I decided to stick my head out the back door, and I see your chonkster of a cat dragging something over the side gate. And Bandit was on the other side, waiting to catch it."

"Fish sticks," I said.

He nodded. "I had a grocery delivery arrive. I was still unpacking it when these two staged their heist."

I rocked back on my heels, mortified. I'd come here to tell Seb off for feeding them, and it turned out the little rascals had stolen an *entire* packet of fish sticks from him. "I am so sorry," I said, wringing my hands. "I can't believe they did that."

Seb laughed. "It's okay, don't be mad. It's kinda funny."

"It is?" I wasn't sure I was there yet. I was stuck halfway between embarrassment and anger.

"Goes to show you have two very intelligent pets," Seb continued. "This took planning."

"And cunning," I added.

"Definitely. But I do apologize. I did, unintentionally, feed your pets."

I waved away his apology. "Don't be silly. It's me who should be apologizing. I'll replace your fish sticks."

"Don't be too hard on them," Seb cajoled. "They really are cute."

"Cute doesn't excuse thievery," I pointed out.

"Also, you might want to check your house."

"Oh? What for?"

"They took an entire packet of fish sticks. I can't see how they could have eaten them all in one sitting, so they may have stashed them somewhere for later. Also, they're meant to be frozen...."

"Oh, my God." I clapped a hand over my mouth, horrified. If they'd hidden the fish sticks individually around the house... oh, this was bad. This was really bad. If I'd thought Thor's farts were rank, imagine days old fish sticks, slowly rotting. I almost threw up in my mouth. "I need to go," I whispered.

"Good luck!" Seb called after me, then, "Oh, wait! We still on for tomorrow night?"

"Oh, about that, sorry, no can do. It's Dad's birthday." I waved an apology and bolted out the front door, across the lawn, and inside my house, skidding down the passageway, sniffing as I went. So far, no smell of rancid fish sticks.

"Thor! Bandit!" I yelled, then paused to listen. Nothing. No furry little paws pounding on the floorboards. I crossed to the back door and stepped onto the deck. Shielding my eyes, I squinted into the afternoon sun. "Thor! Bandit!" I yelled again. Still no response. "Yeah, you wanna hide," I muttered under my breath, "because you're in big trouble."

Ben had yet to return from the old folks' home, so I couldn't quiz him on what he'd found—if anything—on the twelve ghosts who'd greeted me at the door and were now practically up my butt as they followed me throughout the house.

"Why is it that you can't travel to the aged care facility?" I asked them, dodging each and every one as I darted in a bizarre pattern around the living room to get to the coffee machine. I did not like touching ghosts. I tolerated Ben because he was Ben. He was my bestie. But spirits gave me the icy cold shivers, and if I could avoid physical contact, I would.

"Angel," Cecilia answered. It appeared Cecilia was the leader of the pack, the spokesperson, if you will. I glanced at her, and the crowd of ghosts gathered behind her.

"Never mind." It was tough to communicate when all they could say was angel. I turned my attention to the coffee machine, glanced at the clock on the wall. Still seven o'clock. Decided it wasn't too late and proceeded to make myself a cup of caffeine nirvana. While the machine did its thing, I turned to face the ghosts, leaning back against the kitchen counter with my arms crossed. "Did you see where Thor and Bandit stashed the fish sticks?"

"Angel." No head shaking or nodding. I had no idea what it meant. Yes? No? Maybe?

"Could you help me look?" I asked hopefully.

"Angel." Deadpan. Nothing.

"Is that a no?"

"Angel."

"Argh!" I turned my attention back to the coffee machine, ignoring the unhelpful ghosts. "Suppose I'll find those fish sticks when they start stinking up the house." Which reminded me, I still had one puke-filled shoe baking in the sun on the back lawn.

With a certain degree of trepidation, I slid open the back door and cautiously approached the shoe. I peeked inside. Yep, the puke was there. It hadn't evaporated in the sun. But it had dried. Unfortunately for me, it dried like superglue to the innersole. There was nothing for it. The shoe was doomed. I would toss it and treat myself to a new pair as soon as I'd resolved Thor's puking issue.

I heard my phone ringing and knew it was Galloway because Ben had changed the ringtone to *Let's Get It On* by Marvin Gaye. I sprinted up the back stairs, which was a massive miscalculation on my part because my foot caught beneath the rise of the top step and sent me sprawling across the deck. The air whooshed out of my lungs, and my chin hit the deck hard enough to rattle my teeth. In a mad scramble, I crawled to the back door, had just made it over the threshold when the phone stopped ringing. My twelve ghosts were all watching me. I'd like to say with concern, but their faces remained expressionless, which only added insult to injury.

Wincing, I used the doorframe to pull myself upright. With pretty much the entire front of my body throbbing, I hobbled over to my phone and called Galloway back. "Sorry I missed your call," I said breathlessly when he answered. "I was outside, mourning the loss of my shoe."

"Cat puke?"

"Cat puke," I confirmed. "What's up?"

"Just wanted to know if we have an extra guest for dinner tonight?" Galloway asked. "I'm going to pick up take out on the way home and am about to leave. I can grab extra if Seb is joining us?"

"Nope, it's just us."

"What do you want?"

"Surprise me. Oh, and thank you. I'd probably starve if it wasn't for you taking such good care of me."

He laughed. "You've survived this long. I'm sure you'd manage."

After hanging up, I returned to the still open back door. "Thor! Bandit!" I called again. "You are not getting dinner tonight! I know you're full of fish sticks that you STOLE from next door."

I waited a couple of seconds, and sure enough, first one head, then another, popped out from the woods next door.

"What do you mean, no dinner?" Thor demanded, waddling out of the woods and onto the back lawn.

"Hey, Mom!" Bandit chortled, bouncing along beside her bestie.

"I mean exactly what I said," I said to Thor. "No dinner. How many fish sticks did you eat anyway?"

"All of them!" Bandit piped up, and my eyes rounded.

"All of them?" I squeaked. That was... a lot! "Do you have a belly ache?"

"No," they replied in unison, then Thor added, "but they gave me gas for a while." No kidding!

"Where's the bag they were in? You didn't leave it in the woods, did you?"

Bandit reached me first and lifted her paws to my thigh. I absently scratched her ears. "No," she said. "I put it in the garbage like you taught me."

"Good girl." They ate *all* the fish sticks. I couldn't get my head around it. I'd struggle to eat an entire bag of fish sticks in one sitting. How did these two manage it? And what did that mean for, you know, the other end? Were there going to be giant poop explosions? I shuddered at the thought.

"Ouch, what happened to you?" Ben appeared, peering at my face.

I touched my chin, still smarting where I'd connected with the deck. "Tripped up the steps," I told him.

"I think you took some skin off," he said, leaning in closer.

"What?" Alarmed, I hobbled as fast as my aching legs would allow to the bathroom next door to my office and looked in the mirror. "Fan-friggin-tastic." Sure enough, an angry red graze marred my chin and an inch or two along my jaw. "Guess I'm lucky I didn't knock any teeth out."

"It matches the bruise on your forehead."

I'd attempted to hide the bruise under makeup, but since I have a habit of touching my face—a lot—the concealer I'd used had long since worn away.

"Enough about my face." I turned my back on the mirror. "What did you find out? Do we know who this lot is yet?"

Ben punched both fists in the air. "We do. At least I think we do."

"Progress at last!"

"I think I managed to send you an email," Ben said, hiking his thumb toward the office.

The ghosts were hovering in the hallway, and I shooed them away. "Listen," I told them, "we are this close to making a breakthrough. Do you think you can wait in the living room?"

"Angel."

Seems that was a no, for they followed me into the office and crowded in behind me. Wriggling the mouse to wake up the computer, I sat down and opened up my emails. Sure enough, there was one from the Firefly Bay Residential Aged Care Facility. Opening it, I saw a list of names. I glanced at Ben.

"Here we go," I said. "Do we have a Norma Coveny?"

"Angel." A ghost replied behind me.

"Yes," said Ben. "She raised her hand. Keep reading them out."

"Beverley Atkinson?"

"Angel." Another one identified. I went through the entire list. All ghosts present and accounted for.

"How did you manage this?" I asked Ben. "How did you know it was them?"

"They have photographs of the residents on file, so I scoured through the data, searching for faces I recognized."

"Good work."

"They all died within the last three years," Ben said. "In their sleep. Natural causes."

"That part is not so helpful," I grumbled. "Now we know their identities but still don't know why they're here. They died from natural causes. They should have crossed over."

"Unless it wasn't natural causes," Ben pointed out.

I gasped and swung my head to look at him. "You're saying they were all...murdered?"

"Angel," the ghosts yelled, yet again scaring the bejesus out of me.

"Guys!" I shouted back. "We've talked about this. Please! Do not suddenly yell. Especially when you're standing this close." I rubbed my chest. "I don't think my heart can't take any more scares."

"Ha!" Ben laughed and playfully punched my shoulder. It was cold. "You've got plenty of life left in you, Fitz. Ignore her, guys," he said to the ghosts. "We're getting closer to solving the puzzle."

"Are the dates next to the names the day they died?" I drew Ben's attention back to the email he'd sent.

"Yeah. I figured it may be useful to have. I didn't see any pattern, all different dates, different days of the week. The only connection is that they died in their sleep. Supposedly."

Thor and Bandit charged past the office door toward the front of the house with a chorus of, "He's here! He's home!"

"Kade is here," Ben pointed out the obvious, stepping into the hallway and glancing toward the front door. "Oooh, he's brought Chinese. Yum."

Easing out of my chair, I limped into the hallway, almost bumping into Galloway as he swept past.

"Why is it every time I come through that door, you have another bruise or scrape?" Galloway asked, gently tilting my chin to examine the damage before dropping a kiss on the tip of my nose.

"Because I'm—"

"Clumsy." He cut me off. "Yes, I know. Go sit." He pointed to the dining table, and I obliged, taking my sweet time while Galloway unpacked the takeout.

"Here." He placed a glass of water in front of me and two painkillers. I obediently swallowed them and smiled my thanks before piling my plate with egg rolls and chow mein.

"How did it go with the USB?" I asked, mouth full of egg roll.

"How did you do with it?" Galloway grinned, pointing his chopstick at me.

I shrugged. "Not far with the USB, but we did have a breakthrough on the other ghosts."

"Oh?"

"Mmmm. Ben discovered who they are and when they died. They're all past residents of the Firefly Bay Residential Aged Care Facility, and all died in their sleep from apparent natural causes within the last three years."

"Fitz!" Ben shouted from the office.

"What?" I shouted back. Galloway jerked back in his chair, dropping a chopstick. "Sorry," I whispered to him, reaching across the table to touch the back of his hand. "Ben just called me from the office."

"I think I've found something," Ben called out.

"He thinks he's found something," I said to Galloway. "About what?" I shouted to Ben.

"A connection between the data on Molly's USB and our ghost friends here."

I jumped up so fast my chair toppled over backward. I was halfway across the room before the pain in my hips and knees registered, and I slowed my pace. Galloway had righted my chair and was following behind. Collapsing into my office chair, I looked at Ben, who was standing in the middle of the desk with his hand on the computer. On the screen was the file we'd found on Molly's USB.

"Look," I said to Galloway, pointing. "That's the file on Molly's USB."

Galloway walked through the twelve ghosts without even noticing, dragged the spare chair from the corner, and seated himself next to me. "Right," he said.

I looked at Ben. "And?"

"Each number is fourteen digits long, and at first glance, makes zero sense. I haven't been able to match them up to anything. But then I decided to look at them backward, and that's when I realized the last six numbers of the sequence? Those are dates."

"He's saying the last six digits of each of those numbers is a date," I said for Galloway's benefit.

"Agreed. That's what we got as well. The year is abbreviated to two digits, then day, month. It's the eight digits preceding it that we haven't cracked. Yet," Galloway said.

"What he doesn't know, couldn't have known," Ben said with excitement, "is that those dates match the dates our friends here died."

"Oh, my God!" I squeaked, clapping my hands to my face, making my graze sting all over again.

"What is it?" Galloway leaned closer to the screen, trying to see what had gotten me so excited.

"Those dates? They are the dates my ghostly visitors died," I said, tapping the monitor with my finger, making it wobble. "Galloway, we need to get out to the old folks' home and find out what we can about the nights these residents died."

"Angel!" the ghosts agreed.

I was half out of my seat when Galloway placed a hand on my shoulder, holding me down. "Slow down. We're not going tonight. It can wait until morning. We need a warrant. All of this," he waved a hand toward the screen, "has got to be tied in with Molly's murder."

"She discovered that someone was killing the residents!"

"Allegedly. We don't know what she discovered," he pointed out. "What we need to find out is what the rest of these numbers mean."

I slumped in my seat. He had a point. I had half a theory, and while I had Ben's ability to read digital data, I needed Galloway's warrant to make it legal so that whatever charges were eventually laid would stick.

Galloway grinned at me. "I know you hate it when you know I'm right," he teased.

"I so do," I agreed.

"Come on, let's finish dinner, then I'm thinking a long soak in the tub and an early night. I'll put a rush on that warrant, and we can go in the morning, providing the judge doesn't mind being disturbed on a Sunday."

"Would you be joining me in the tub?" I asked hopefully. His answering grin could only be described as wolfish. My heart flip-flopped in my chest in anticipation. "Come on then, let's eat!"

Chapter Fourteen

"Where should we start?" I asked, standing by Galloway's side in the foyer of the Firefly Bay Residential Aged Care Facility. Turns out the judge had been in a good mood, and Galloway now had the warrant in hand. He'd presented it at reception, and the Facility's Medical Director had been alerted to our presence.

"*We* aren't starting anywhere," Galloway pointed out. "Officers Walsh and Jacobs, however, are going to start—"

"In the treatment room?" I suggested. Because from where I was standing, I could see the treatment room, and I remembered seeing the drug cabinet the last time I visited. And Dean had access. I lowered my voice. "Dean Ackerman has a bad back," I said. "Both his girlfriend and wife mentioned him popping pain pills."

"An excellent starting point, but remember, we follow the evidence. We don't make the evidence fit the suspect."

"Gotcha."

Technically, as Galloway had reminded me, I wasn't allowed to partake in the search. That was left to Officer Noah Walsh and Officer Sarah Jacobs, who hadn't batted an eye when I'd arrived with Galloway. From time to time, Galloway allowed me to assist on cases under the guise of a consultant. Today was one of those occasions. It helped that he had been my supervisor when I was training to be a PI.

Surprisingly, once they'd started looking, it didn't take them long to discover what Molly had. The six digits at the start of her code represented different drugs. There was a code for opioids, another for sedatives, and another for morphine. And there were discrepancies with all three drugs. Someone had gone to a lot of trouble to hide the fact that drugs were missing.

"Excuse me." A man in a suit appeared in the doorway of the treatment room. "I'm David Boyer, Medical Director. Can I be of assistance?" He had a full head of gray hair, yet despite appearing to be in his sixties, he had a distinct lack of wrinkles and a frozen expression. This guy was botoxed up the wazoo. His hands gave him away though, the dry papery skin with age spots belied his age.

"I'm going to need you to step back." Galloway approached, putting himself between me and the MD. "I'm Detective Galloway. This is Officers Walsh and Jacobs and Audrey Fitzgerald."

David's eyes skimmed over us before zeroing in on Galloway. He held up his hands and took two steps back into the corridor. "Sorry."

"Not a problem." Galloway gave a curt nod and pulled out his phone, swiping to his note app. "Who has access to this room?"

"All nursing and cleaning staff."

"And to the drug cabinet?" Galloway jerked his thumb toward the cabinet that now stood open. The top portion housed boxes of various medications. The bottom was refrigerated and held vials of what appeared to be insulin and morphine and possibly some vaccines at the back.

"Oh, that would be the Nurse Assessment Coordinator and the registered nurses. All medications have to be double-checked prior to administration."

"Double-checked by who?"

"The RN would typically draw up the medication as per the resident's chart, and a nurse would check that the dosage is correct."

"And who fills out the register?"

"The RN."

"I'm going to need a list of all your RNs. That's registered nurse, correct?"

David gave a curt nod, his eyes darting around the room, keeping a keen eye on what the officers were doing.

"And when was the last audit?" Galloway asked.

"For the pharmaceuticals? I'd have to double-check that for you. I don't have the information on hand."

"Right." Galloway handed him a card. "If you can forward all of that to this email address at your earliest convenience."

"Is all this really necessary?" David sniffed, waving a hand in the air.

"One of your employees was murdered," Galloway said. "I would have thought you'd be invested in finding out what happened to her."

"Molly Lewis was a nursing assistant. She did not have access to pharmaceuticals; therefore, I fail to see why you need that information from us." David's voice was defensive and whiney.

"Molly may not have had access, but her killer could have," Galloway shot back, and if

David's eyebrows could have moved, I'd imagine they would have risen into his hairline. Come to think of it, were they plugs? I squinted and shuffled closer for a better look. Yes! Definitely plugs.

"I'm sure I don't need to remind you, Mr. Boyer, that this is a police investigation, and we have a warrant. If I discover you have been withholding information, you may be charged with hindering an investigation."

David's eyes narrowed to mere slits. "I'll get my assistant to send you the information you requested." He swiveled on his heel and stalked away.

"What a friendly chap," I piped up from behind Galloway.

He shrugged and turned to face me. "Plugs?" he asked.

"Definitely." I nodded.

"We'll get pathology to cross-match the sedatives missing and those that were found in Molly's system," Galloway said, watching as Officers Walsh and Jacobs photographed and logged everything.

"And Dean?" I prompted.

"I'll organize a search warrant for his home." Galloway had his phone in his hand and started to dial. I stepped out of the treatment room and basically loitered in the hallway. I knew the search wouldn't end with the treatment room. The warrant gave the officers carte blanche over the facility except for residents' rooms. I presumed we'd be here all day.

"What's going on?" Sharon Mooney approached, eyebrows drawn together as her eyes darted to the crowded treatment room and back to me.

"Search warrant," I explained.

"Really?" Her voice went up three octaves. "Why?"

"Molly's death wasn't an accident. They found sedatives in her system."

Sharon's eyes narrowed much like David Boyer's had. "And the police think they came from here?"

I shrugged. "That's what they need to find out. Molly worked here. Coincidentally, or not, you have drugs here."

"Yes, but Molly doesn't. Didn't," she corrected herself, "have access to them." Sharon's tone was indignant, as if she took it as a personal affront that we'd suspect Molly of stealing drugs.

I cocked my head and studied Sharon. She looked worse than ever. Haggard. Showing every one of her sixty years and then some. "I hardly think Molly stole sedatives, then took them—with alcohol—and then got behind the wheel," I said.

Sharon paused, and I could practically see the cogs turning. "Oh. Do you think someone else slipped her the sedative without her knowledge? But why?"

"That's what we're trying to figure out."

She rubbed her shoulder and glanced back at the treatment room, watching as the officers pulled everything out of the cupboards. "They're very thorough," she muttered, more to herself than to me.

"Mmmm," I agreed.

Sharon was chewing on her bottom lip, brow furrowed.

"Everything okay?" I reached out and touched her shoulder, snatching my hand back when she winced.

"Sorry," she grimaced. "Bursitis in my shoulder has flared up again. My own silly fault. I rearranged the furniture in my living room, and the sofa was heavier than it looked."

"Ouch, my dad had that, pretty uncomfortable," I commiserated, not really paying attention to Sharon's ailments but what was going on in the treatment room. Drugs were missing, and I was ninety-nine percent sure Dean Ackerman was the thief and possibly Molly's killer. Molly knowing about his affair was a flimsy motive, but Molly discovering he'd been stealing drugs? That was a motive to kill.

Everything was falling into place. Molly's code. It was morphine going missing on the dates my ghosts had died. The ghosts continually saying angel? I'd finally figured out what they meant. They were trying to tell me that the Firefly Bay Residential Aged

Care Facility had an Angel of Mercy. Someone—Dean—was killing residents as a perceived act of mercy, putting them out of their apparent misery.

Galloway called my name, waving his phone. Sharon hurried off with a hasty farewell and something about an ice pack.

"You got the warrant already?" I asked, surprised at how fast he'd made it happen.

"Yep. We'll leave Walsh and Jacobs to continue on here. You and I will search Ackerman's house. It's looking worse and worse for that guy."

* * *

Dean and Katherine Ackerman were home when we arrived with the search warrant. I'm guessing Galloway had to pull in some favors with the judge to get him signing warrants on a weekend.

"What's this about?" Dean sputtered, shifting from one foot to the other, his face pale.

"The death of Molly Lewis," Galloway said, thrusting the warrant at him when he refused to take it.

"What?" Dean choked. "I didn't kill Molly. I swear! Why would I?"

Galloway arched a brow. "You really want me to go into it here, in front of your wife?"

Dean cast a frantic glance at Katherine, who was standing by his side, utterly confused. Poor woman, I felt for her.

"Look." Dean lowered his voice. "Despite what you may think, I did not kill Molly Lewis. I have no motive." Besides Molly finding out about his affair with a co-worker, that is.

"And he has an alibi," Katherine piped up. "He was at work."

So he says. While Dean's schedule put him at work, I still needed to confirm with coworkers that he was actually there and not off canoodling with Angela. I was kicking myself that I didn't take the opportunity to do that while Galloway and his officers were conducting the search. A perfect opportunity missed.

"If you could take a seat on the couch, please." Galloway ushered them into the living room. "This shouldn't take long." Snapping on a pair of latex gloves, Galloway headed down the hallway peering into rooms as he went, looking for the bathroom. I'd already given him the heads up that Ben had seen pharmaceuticals in the bathroom cabinet. Having a ghost best friend had its advantages.

"Hands in pockets," Galloway instructed me, and I dutifully stuffed my hands into the back pockets of my jeans so I wouldn't be tempted to touch anything. I waited in the doorway while Galloway headed straight for the cabinet. Sure enough, a shelf full of medications greeted him.

He picked up a container of pills and read the label. "Dimethyl fumarate. Prescription. Made out to Katherine Ackerman."

"She has MS," I said. "That's why she only works a few hours a week because she gets tired quickly, and that can trigger a relapse."

"Right." He nodded and put the pill container back. Next was a foil strip with a row of pills on each side. Galloway held it up and squinted at it. "OxyContin," he read. He placed it on the vanity and picked up a partially empty blister pack, slightly different from the first. "Temazepam," he read.

"Those are the pain killers and sleeping pills missing from the aged care facility," I confirmed.

"Yeah, but not in great quantities. And there's nothing to prove these are stolen. They could be legit, providing Ackerman can prove he had a script for them."

"How much are we looking for?" I asked. All I knew was that drugs were missing.

"He was clever. He took a blister pack from multiple boxes, always keeping the ones at the front full, so no one realized the boxes at the back didn't contain the correct amount," he added.

"Until Molly did an audit." But she didn't have direct access to the drugs cabinet, someone would have had to unlock it for her.

If that someone was Dean, he would have put her off, somehow, or volunteered to help so he could fudge the numbers.

Galloway nodded. "That's if it was Dean." He continued rummaging through the bathroom cabinet, then moved on to the vanity. He picked up a tissue box, gave it a cursory shake as he moved it out of the way, then froze.

"Hear that?" he asked.

"Sounds like more than tissues in there." I eased closer, eager to see. Galloway pulled out a wad of tissues, and there, in the bottom of the tissue box, were at least a dozen blister packs. "Bingo."

Pulling an evidence bag from his back pocket, he dropped the strips inside. "Let's go see what he has to say."

Dean and Katherine were sitting side by side on the sofa, holding hands. I'd have said it looked cute if it weren't for the fact that Dean was a cheating weasel with a drug habit.

"Care to explain these?" Galloway asked, holding the bag aloft.

"What are they?" Katherine asked.

"OxyContin and Temazepam," Galloway said. "Stolen from the Firefly Bay Residential Aged Care Facility."

"What?" Katherine gasped, turning to face her husband. "Dean?"

He crumbled. Really, this guy had no backbone. I'm amazed he had the balls to not only steal drugs but carry out multiple affairs, for when confronted, he caved immediately.

"Okay, okay, I admit it." He released his wife's hand to throw his arms in the air. "I have a bad back. The doctor refused to prescribe any more pain relief, and I needed it. *Needed* it." His voice rose, and his foot tapped, his whole leg jerking. "And there it was, just sitting in the drug cabinet at work. No one would notice if I took a strip or two."

"This is more than a strip or two," Galloway pointed out.

"I'd say you have an addiction, Dean," I added. He shot to his feet and took a threatening step toward me.

"I do not!" he yelled. "I'm not an addict!"

Galloway stepped in front of me and pointed at Dean. "Sit! Now!" His voice rang with authority. Katherine sat wide-eyed, looking from her husband to Galloway and back again.

Dean subsided like a deflated balloon next to her. "I'm sorry," he mumbled.

"And you needed the Temazepam to help you sleep?" Galloway asked.

Dean shook his head. "No. That's for Katherine."

"What?" She looked at her husband in shock. He turned to her, his face full of love and sadness.

"I'm sorry," he whispered, eyes filling with tears. "I'm so sorry."

"What's going on?" she cried.

"Were you slipping sedatives to your wife without her knowledge?" Galloway asked, and I remembered then what Katherine had told me. That Dean would make her a cup of tea before heading out. That time when she'd been watching her favorite soap, and he'd given her a cup of tea, and then she'd been so sleepy she'd gone to bed early. Because there had been Temazepam in her tea.

Dean nodded, and Katherine started to cry.

"And the morphine?" Galloway prompted. "Where's that? If I were to search your fridge, would I find it?"

"What? No way! I don't do morphine. I haven't touched it. I swear I haven't stolen any morphine from work. Go check!"

"I intend to." Galloway spent the next few minutes searching the refrigerator while I stayed with the Ackermans, watching as Dean tried to comfort Katherine, who was confused and hurt about what she'd learned about her husband. But she hadn't asked the question I was waiting for her to ask. Or maybe she suspected what the answer would be and didn't want to know, didn't want it confirmed that her husband dosed her tea so she wouldn't notice he'd been cheating on her. Way to cover your tracks when you stayed out late or left for work early.

"I swear to God," Dean said to me, "I did not take any morphine. I just needed the oxy. The sedatives were for Katherine, to help her sleep."

"Sure." I shrugged, not believing him.

"Look!" He stood up and held both arms out to me. "No track marks. I'm not using morphine. I have no need to steal it."

"Junkies don't just inject their arms," I pointed out.

"I'm not a junkie!" he protested vehemently.

"You're an addict. Just because it's a prescription medication doesn't make you less of an addict."

"Okay, fine." He sat back down. "I'm an addict. I'm an oxy addict. Not morphine. I don't do injectables."

"Nothing there." Galloway returned. "I believe him. I don't think he took the morphine."

"How much is missing?" Dean asked.

"I'm not at liberty to say."

"What happens now?" Katherine asked, eyes bloodshot, nose red.

"I send these to the lab to confirm they match what is missing from Dean's employer. You can expect charges to be made. In the meantime, don't leave town."

Dean and Katherine nodded soberly while we let ourselves out.

Back in the car, I turned to Galloway. "So, Molly was right. Dean was stealing drugs."

"Yeah, it looks that way. Trouble is, Dean has a rock-solid alibi. At the time of her death, he was at work."

"You beat me to it," I said. "You sure he didn't duck out for a little tryst on his break or something?"

Galloway shook his head. "Times don't match up. Co-workers put Dean at the facility. He took his break in the break room, didn't leave until his shift ended."

"And that must have been when he went to visit Angela. In between finishing work and going home."

"Her alibi holds too. She was also on nights and was there the entire time."

"So, who the heck killed Molly?" I asked. "Dean definitely has motive. Molly knew about the affair, and she knew about the missing drugs."

"But did she know it was Dean who stole them?" Galloway asked. "She was smart enough to record her findings as a code, yet there is nothing in that code to tell us she suspected Dean was the culprit."

I snapped my fingers. "I've been looking at it all wrong," I declared. "Molly wasn't focusing on the missing drugs—not directly. What she was trying to prove was that someone was killing residents. Someone considers themselves an Angel of Mercy, putting the residents out of their perceived misery. And I'm guessing because the deaths were all listed as natural causes, no autopsies were ever carried out."

"I can double-check that."

"The bodies probably weren't examined at all, which meant no-one would have been looking for an injection site."

"You think he used the morphine to overdose them?"

"Well, he isn't going to wake them up and say, '*Here, you forgot to take your meds. Can you just swallow these six pills*?' All the deaths happened at night. All we have to do is check the rosters. I bet Dean Ackerman was working the nights they died, and Molly was about to expose him."

"Still doesn't explain how he managed to be in two places at once," Galloway said. "At work and killing Molly."

"Yeah. I'm still working on that." How, indeed, did Dean do it?

Chapter Fifteen

"Good news, my spectral friends," I told the twelve ghosts when Galloway dropped me off at home. For the first time *ever*, they'd stayed put hovering in the middle of my living room. I pinched together my thumb and forefinger. "I'm this close to solving your case."

"Angel?" they chorused.

"Angel means Angel of Mercy, right?" I asked.

"Angel." They nodded.

"Someone gave you a morphine overdose the night you died."

"Angel," they concurred.

"Only, of course, you were asleep. You wouldn't have seen who. But you knew that your passing wasn't natural. It was drug-induced. Which is why you've been hanging around. Where have you been all this time?" I asked on a tangent. "Hanging out at the home?"

"Angel."

"Right. Never mind, doesn't matter. One of the RNs, Dean Ackerman, was helping himself to the drug cabinet like its personal pharmacy. All we have to do now is match up his roster to the nights you died, and bingo, we have our man. Or angel. Although I don't want to call him an angel because that makes it sound like he's doing good, worthy things, and he's not. He's deluded."

"Uh, Fitz?" Ben interrupted.

"Yeah?"

He pointed to the back door, and I turned to find Seb standing there, watching me through the glass.

"Holy crapadoodles," I whispered. "Did he just witness…"

"He did."

"I can bluff my way through this." I straightened my shoulders and crossed to the door, sliding it open. "Seb!" I greeted. "What can I do for you?"

"I've worked it out," Seb said, stepping over the threshold, his eyes scanning the living room as if he could see the twelve ghosts and Ben.

"Oh?" I headed to the coffee machine. "Coffee?"

"Sure." Seb pulled up a seat at the breakfast bar. "You talk to the dead, don't you?"

The cup I'd been holding slipped through my fingers and shattered on the floor.

"Hey, it's okay!" Seb cried, hurrying around the breakfast bar to begin picking up shards of broken crockery while I stood in dumbfounded shock. "I'm not going to tell anyone. And I don't think you're a freak," he added, glancing up at me. "What happened to your chin?"

I touched the graze. "Tripped coming up the deck steps," I said absently. I was kinda frozen in a combination of disbelief and horror. He'd guessed the truth, and now was the do or die moment. Confess or perpetuate the lie. I looked over to Ben, who shrugged.

"So, who is it? Who's here?" Seb asked, carrying the broken shards over to the bin and dumping them inside. He snapped his fingers and pointed at me, as excited as a kid in a candy store. "I know, I know, it's your friend! The one who used to live here. He's haunting the place, right?"

"I wouldn't say haunting," Ben grumbled, and before I could engage my brain to tell my mouth to shut up, I'd replied, "He doesn't like the term haunting."

Ben barked out a laugh. "Truth's out there now, Fitz."

"Fair enough. So, he still lives here? Although could we call it living when he's, you know, not?" Seb continued on as if I hadn't just let slip that yes, I was talking to the ghost of my best friend.

"He's here, yes." There. I'd said it. Now I had to trust that Seb would stay true to his word.

I crossed my fingers behind my back as if that would help.

"This is so cool." Seb rubbed his hands together, then caught sight of the trepidation that had to be written all over my face. "I swear, I won't breathe a word. I promise." He made a cross over his heart. "Does anyone else know?"

"Galloway," I confessed. "Please don't say anything. I don't want folks knowing I can talk to ghosts, okay?" Even though he'd already promised, I needed to hear it again.

"Cross my heart and hope to die," Seb said solemnly.

"Good enough for me!" Ben declared, and I gave him a weak smile.

"I'd better not be making a colossal mistake," I said to Seb, reaching into the overhead cupboard for another cup.

"You haven't. I am, if anything, a man of my word. So, how goes the case?" He resumed his seat. "Does your friend—what's his name anyway?—help with your cases?"

"His name is Ben, and yes, he helps. Once upon a time, he was a Firefly Bay Police Department member, then he became a Private Investigator. Delaney Investigations was his business."

Seb propped his chin on one hand and hung on every word while I found myself filling him in on Molly's case and the twelve ghosts who were now standing behind him unabashedly admiring his good looks. I figured if they approved of him, then I had nothing to worry about.

"So, what's next?" Seb asked when I'd finished bringing him up to speed.

"Galloway is sending over the rosters. All I have to do is confirm that Dean was working on each of the nights the residents died, and boom, we have our killer."

"But that doesn't prove he killed Molly," Seb pointed out.

"I know. I'm hoping he'll crack under pressure and confess." It was a reasonable supposition, considering Dean had caved as soon as we'd put the hard word on him earlier. Seb was nodding by my side.

"What brought you over here in the first place?" I asked.

"Oh!" He clapped his hands together. "Thor barfing? I think I have the answer."

"Really? What?"

"There is a big potted plant on my back porch," Seb began, "that has the distinct imprint of something, or should I say someone, using it as a bed. The gray fur also gave me a massive clue as to who the culprit might be."

"Oh, good grief! Thor has been sleeping on your plants?"

Seb shrugged. "Hey, no skin off my nose, it's not my plant. It got left behind when the previous resident moved out."

I decided I'd hold off telling Seb about Mrs. Hill. Plenty of time to fill him in on the homicidal old lady who used to live there.

"Anyway, I thought I'd look up what type of plant it is because, you know, Thor's clearly been sleeping on it, and I wondered if maybe—"

"Maybe it was toxic?" I cut in, following his train of thought.

"Exactly!"

"And?"

"It's a chrysanthemum, and chrysanthemum flowers are mildly toxic to cats. Pollen from the flowers would have transferred to his fur and when he groomed himself—"

"He ingested it. Making him sick," I finished.

"Well whadda ya know," Ben drawled. "Looks like we've got another detective on our hands."

"Right?" I grinned.

Seb looked around. "You were talking to Ben, right?"

"Yes, sorry. He says you're quite the detective."

Seb gave a toss of his head and smoothed his fingers over invisible lapels. "Why, thank you. I try." He eased off the barstool and stretched. "Anyway, I must get going. I just wanted to tell you that I've cut all the flowers off the chrysanthemum, so you shouldn't have any more trouble with cat vomit."

"Thank you. And thank you for the other stuff too." I walked him to the door.

"No problemo." He waved. "Good luck with the case, Becket."

"Take care, Castle."

After he'd gone, I turned to Ben. "Well? Did I just make a mistake?"

"What, trusting Seb? Nah, I think he'll be true to his word. I like him."

"Me too. It will suck if he turns out to be an untrustworthy jerk."

"Angel," the ghosts intoned.

Rubbing my hands together, I headed toward my office. "Right. Galloway said he'd email through the spreadsheet with the schedules for the last three years. You wanna help?"

"By help, you mean you want me to do it for you," Ben said, trailing along by my side.

"Of course!" I declared. "Because I have an idea."

"And now you have a headache?" Ben teased.

"Har har." I smacked his shoulder, almost throwing myself to the floor. Staggering, I regained my balance. "No. While you go through the schedules, I'm going to trace Molly's steps from the night she died."

"You don't think Galloway's already done that?"

I shrugged. "Probably. But they haven't made any arrests, so I'm guessing they haven't come up with anything. Molly was meeting someone the night she died. She had alcohol in her system. That leads me to believe they met at a pub or bar."

"Or the killer's house."

"But if that were the case, why the elaborate car crash? Why not kill her in your home and dispose of the body some other way? That's what I'd do. Overdose her, shove her body in the trunk, and go bury her in the woods."

"Should I be worried?" Ben asked.

"What? Of me killing you? A bit late for that."

"That you didn't even have to stop and pause on how you'd perform the perfect murder."

"Pft. That's not perfect. I'm sure I could come up with something better if I took the time to sit down and plan it properly. Which also tells me that whoever killed Molly was in a hurry. Their plan was thrown together, and a lot of it relied on pure luck. Molly might not have died in the crash. What if she survived and told someone who she was with and what they'd done?"

I'd spent all afternoon on a non-alcoholic pub crawl and had turned up nothing. No one I spoke to remembered seeing Molly. I'd shown Dean's photo around as well. No luck. So much for my bright idea. I dropped into the station with a heavy heart and a full bladder to visit Galloway before heading home.

"Any luck with the schedules?" he asked when I appeared in his doorway.

"Ben's looking at them. I haven't heard from him, so I assume no news yet." I shifted my weight from leg to leg.

"You okay?" Galloway asked, watching me.

"I need to pee," I admitted. I'd had a soda at each pub, some misguided idea that if I bought a drink from each place I visited, they'd be more inclined to talk to me. That strategy hadn't worked, and now I was practically vibrating from the sugar rush, and my bladder wanted a stern word with me. "I'll be back in a second." I hurried off to take care of business.

"Better?" Galloway asked when I returned.

"Much. So," I plopped down into the chair opposite his desk, "I've visited every drinking establishment I can think of to see if anyone saw Molly the night she died. No luck."

"The problem is, it was a Thursday evening," Galloway said. "Thursday, Friday, and Saturday nights are the busiest for most pubs and bars."

"And?"

"If I were planning on meeting someone for nefarious purposes, I'd choose the busiest bar at the busiest time. No one's going to notice you. The bartender won't remember you, so long as you go under the radar and don't do anything that draws attention."

"But wouldn't dragging a half-unconscious person out of a bar draw attention?"

"Exactly." He nodded. "We think whoever Molly was with suggested leaving the bar before the sedative they'd slipped into her drink took effect. They knew how long it would take to kick in and how long they had to get Molly to her car before she collapsed."

"And therefore not attract attention." Smart of the killer and smart of Galloway to figure it out. "Tell me you have CCTV footage from the busiest pub in town?"

He grinned. "I have CCTV footage from the three most popular bars. Only it will take time to go through it all. We've started, but the situation at the Firefly Bay Residential Aged Care Facility has taken resources away."

I leaned back in my chair and crossed my legs. "I have just the answer for that."

"Oh?"

"Email them to me. Ben can scour through the footage for us."

Galloway tapped a pen against his lips. "You know, that's not a bad idea. I'll wrap up here for the day and spend the rest of the afternoon at your place—we have dinner with your folks tonight, right?"

"We do." I had yet to work out how I would hide the graze on my chin from my family. Makeup would take care of the bruise on my forehead, providing I didn't rub at it all evening, but the graze was another matter. Not that I was worried what my parents would say—they are used to my scrapes and tumbles. No. It was my sister-in-law, Amanda. I know her concern comes from a place of love, but man, her quest to fix me had become tiresome, and at the moment, we were in the middle of a truce. As soon as she saw the scrape, I suspected all truces would be off, and she'd be back to her meddling self.

Chapter Sixteen

"Ah good, you're back," Ben greeted us when Galloway and I arrived home.

"News on the schedules?" I asked, dumping my bag on the hallway table and heading into the office while Galloway continued to the kitchen. "It was Dean Ackerman, wasn't it?"

"Bad news, I'm afraid," Ben said, and I paused from where I'd been leaning over the desk to squint at the monitor to shoot him a look over my shoulder.

"Bad news?" I echoed.

Ben shrugged. "Dean Ackerman was not on duty the nights our friends here died."

I eased into the chair, deflated. I'd been so sure it had been Dean.

"Who then?" I asked.

"I'm still working on that. I've got three years of schedules to go through. It's going to take a little time."

"How much time?"

He shrugged again. "It was easier when I was only crossmatching Dean. After all, we both thought he was our guy. But now that I don't have a suspect, I'm going to have to cross-match all the staff and then filter through who has access to the morphine."

"Tell Ben about the CCTV footage!" Galloway interrupted with a shout from the kitchen.

"You have more footage?" Ben asked, ears pricked.

"Yeah. We're going to have to shelve our resident ghosts for the moment and focus on Molly. Galloway's emailed video files of the footage from three different pubs taken the night Molly died. We think she was at one of those pubs with her killer. Could you work your magic and see what you can find?"

"Sure thing." Ben flexed his fingers and waited while I opened the email, then he plunged his hand into the computer. The screen flickered and shimmered as Ben's spectral energy zipped along the digital pathways. He closed his eyes and concentrated on reading the data.

I left him to it, joining Galloway in the kitchen. "I should probably tell you about a... development that happened this morning," I said.

"Oh?"

"Mmmm. Seb caught me talking to the ghosts, and he guessed. He guessed I could see—and communicate—with the dead."

Galloway paused mid stir of his coffee, face thoughtful. "And I take it you confirmed that guess? That's why you have this guilty look on your face?"

I chewed my lip and tried not to look sheepish. I somehow think I failed cos Galloway chuckled. "It's okay, Audrey, you can tell whoever you like. It's your business, not mine."

"Yes, but...I don't want people to know." The more people who knew, the bigger risk that word would eventually get out, and the entire town would think I was a nut case.

"I think Seb is going to be a good friend." Galloway handed me his coffee. "Take this. You look like you need it more than me. I'll make another."

"I love you." I took the coffee and wrapped both hands around the mug.

"You talking to me or the coffee?"

"Both."

"Guys!" Ben yelled from the office.

"Coming!" I said, moving as fast as I could without spilling my coffee, adding for Galloway's benefit, "Ben has something."

"Whatcha got?" I asked, taking my seat and rubbing my cheek against Galloway's arm when he stood behind me and rested a hand on my shoulder.

"Found her. She was at The Bay. Not a good shot, though. She's in the back." The video was frozen on the monitor, and Ben pointed to a pixelated and fuzzy figure.

"She's here," I said for Galloway's benefit, leaning forward and tapping the screen.

"Hit play," Galloway said, and I dutifully clicked play on the video. We watched as the last footage of Molly alive played out on the screen. Because she was in the background, the clarity wasn't great, but I recognized the bright floral top Galloway had described and her brown curly hair.

"Who's she with?" I squinted. I could see the other figure, but again, the picture wasn't clear.

"Well, it's not Ackerman," Galloway said. "The build is way too small. I think she's with a woman."

"Angela?" I'd ruled out Molly's best friend as a suspect, but maybe I'd been wrong. "But didn't she have an alibi?"

"It's not Angela," Galloway said emphatically. "Angela's taller and slimmer than this woman."

"Katherine?" I guessed.

"No."

"Who *is* that?" I leaned closer, watching as Molly stood and left the pub together with her mystery companion. Something niggled at the back of my mind. The way the other woman moved. I recognized that walk. But I couldn't put my finger on who, exactly, it was, and since we didn't have a clear shot of her face, we were still none-the-wiser as to who Molly was with that night.

"You know, don't you?" Ben said, watching me. I squeezed my eyes shut, trying to remember.

"I can't quite place her," I said. "I know the walk. She reminds me of someone, but the memory is just out of reach."

"Don't force it," Galloway warned, squeezing my shoulder. "Move over. I'm going to send this on to our tech guys and see if they can't sharpen the image for us."

I left Galloway sitting at my desk while I settled on the sofa. Thor squeezed himself through the cat door, back legs suspended in the air while he wriggled his belly through.

"Is it dinner time?" he asked, perusing his horrifyingly empty bowl. The vet had warned me not to keep a constant supply of kibble available for my plump puss. He now got a measured dose every morning and afternoon, and, despite his protests to the contrary, he wasn't actually starving.

"No."

For once, Thor didn't have a snarky comeback. Instead, he ambled across the room and jumped up onto the sofa next to me. Bandit burst through the cat door seconds later, spilling into the room with a clatter of claws on the floor. "Hey, Mom!" she chortled. I loved how she was such a happy little camper.

"How are your bellies today? After yesterday's fish sticks?" I asked.

Thor, who was pressed up against my thigh and purring, didn't even look at me. "No problems."

"Thor said his butthole was on fire," Bandit chimed in, making herself comfortable next to Thor.

I snorted. "He did?"

"He said he'd never pooped so much in his life!" she confided.

"Oh, really?" I laughed even harder. I can only imagine that overindulging in fish sticks resulted in a less than pleasant experience with them coming out the other end. I was grateful he hadn't vomited them up in my shoes.

Running a hand over Thor's back, I was rewarded with a louder purr. "No more stealing food from Seb, okay? And good news, we know what was making you sick. The flowers you were sleeping on in the pot on Seb's back porch—they aren't good for cats."

"But I like sleeping there," Thor said, his voice slow with drowsiness.

"Lucky for you, Seb isn't that worried about you sleeping on his plant. He's cut the flowers off, so you shouldn't be bothered by them, but how come you've taken to sleeping there now? You never did when Mrs. Hill lived there."

"Mrs. Hill had that stupid dog, Percy."

"I thought you liked Percy?"

"I liked to wind him up," Thor corrected. "But it was impossible to sleep with him constantly yapping in your face."

"I like Percy," Bandit piped up.

"You never even met him," Thor drawled with a yawn.

"Who's Percy?" Bandit asked.

"He's a pug dog who used to live next door," I explained. "Thor liked to tease him."

"Audrey?" Galloway called from the office. "Is Ben doing something to the computer? It's doing funny things."

"Yeah, sorry, that's me!" Ben called back. "I'll stop."

"Oh, it's okay, it's stopped now," Galloway informed me.

Ben joined me, Thor, and Bandit in the living room. "What were you doing?" I asked him.

"I was having another go at the schedules," he said. "But I'll wait until Kade has finished sending his email."

"Tell Ben I'm finishing up now!" Galloway yelled from the office. It was uncanny how he picked up on what we were saying despite not hearing Ben. Even as I was thinking it, Galloway appeared in the doorway. "All done," he said.

"Great." Ben jumped up and walked through the office wall to continue his perusal of the schedules.

"Hey, Thor, buddy." Galloway scratched Thor's ears, then Bandit's, with a crooned, "How you doing, beautiful?" as he settled at the other end of the sofa, balancing his coffee on the arm.

"Ben is working on the schedules," I explained. Crammed in behind the sofa were the twelve ghosts.

"Fitz!" Ben bellowed. It wasn't his usual yell. This one held a distinct tone of triumph.

Leaning forward, I placed my coffee on the table and stood, doing my best not to disturb Thor. "He's got something," I said to Galloway. The twelve ghosts beat me to the office, which was a first.

"Have you found them?" I asked, standing in the doorway, not wanting to squeeze past the ghosts jammed into my office.

"It's Sharon Mooney," Ben said.

I blinked in surprise. "Sharon? As in, the older lady with the gray hair?"

"Sixty is not that old, Fitz," Ben said. "But yes. Her."

"How did you discover that so quickly? You said it was going to take a while because you had to cross-reference all the staff."

"The footage from The Bay showed Molly was with a woman, so I narrowed down my parameters. Female staff members with access to the drug cabinet. That shortened the list considerably. Then I just had to cross-reference those names with who was on duty each night a death occurred. Sharon Mooney is the only one. It has to be her."

I repeated what Ben had said for Galloway's benefit. "Bring up the footage again, the CCTV," I demanded. Galloway, who'd taken my seat at the desk, did so. He fast-forwarded to the time stamp where Molly and her killer were leaving, then hit play.

"That's why she looked familiar. The way she walks. That," I pointed to the monitor, "is Sharon Mooney." Despite not seeing her face, the way she favored one leg, the way her hips rolled as she moved—I recognized it from the time I'd watched Sharon walk away from me at the Firefly Bay Residential Aged Care Facility. Never in a million years would I have suspected her of Molly's death. "How on earth did she drag Molly out of the car?" I wondered out loud, then gasped and clapped a hand over my mouth.

"What is it?" Galloway swiveled in his seat.

"Sharon has a bad shoulder! She said it's bursitis, that it flared up after moving her furniture around."

"More likely dragging a body around," Ben said.

Galloway checked his watch. "We've got time."

"Time?"

"Before dinner with your folks for your dad's birthday," he said. "We have time to arrest a killer."

Chapter Seventeen

"Sharon Mooney, I'm arresting you for the murder of Molly Lewis." Galloway nodded to Sergeant Addison Young and Officer Tom Collier, who'd met us at the aged care facility.

"What?" she sputtered. "That's ridiculous. It wasn't me."

"We have CCTV footage of you at The Bay with Molly the night she died."

Sharon looked from me to Galloway and back again. I'd been expecting Sharon to maintain her staunch stand that she was innocent, so when she threw her hands in the air and declared, "Fine! I did it. Arrest me," and held her wrists out to be cuffed, you could have blown me down with a feather.

"Why did you kill her?" I blurted, unable to contain the question.

Her shoulders slumped as she dropped her arms to her sides, and her whole body rolled forward, hunched, defeated. "Molly came to me saying she'd discovered something terrible, that there were discrepancies with the number of OxyContin and Temazepam we had on hand. I knew it was only a matter of time before she discovered the morphine."

"And it was you?" Galloway prompted. "Stealing the morphine? Did you use it to overdose the residents in your care?"

"I provide a service!" Sharon straightened, thrusting her chest out, chin lifting. "These people need me. They need me to help them. I save them from a long, drawn-out, painful death. They need me," she repeated, so sure of herself, so confident that what she'd done had been the right thing.

"And you decided you needed to kill Molly too?" Galloway prompted.

"She was about to ruin everything." Sharon pouted. "I told her it was too risky to discuss at work, that we should meet at The Bar, but she shouldn't tell anyone it was me she was meeting, that she should say she's going out with her boyfriend."

"I slipped the Temazepam into her drink, then lured her out to her car. It wasn't hard.

It was noisy in the pub. We had to raise our voices, and I simply suggested we didn't want anyone to overhear us. By the time we got to the parking lot, the Temazepam was kicking in—I gave her a good dose—and it took hardly any effort to get Molly into the passenger seat. She was semi-conscious and didn't know what was happening. I told her she wasn't well, and I'd drive her home."

"But you didn't drive her home." Galloway crossed his arms. "You drove her into a tree."

Sharon nodded. "I did."

"That was a heck of a risk. Molly might not have died. You could have been seriously injured."

Sharon reflexively raised a hand to her shoulder. Galloway's eyes followed the movement. "Hurt your shoulder, huh? I bet you've got some bruised ribs to go with that, hmm? Having an airbag go off can do that."

"Just bruised, nothing broken," Sharon admitted.

"Why did you even put the seatbelt on Molly? Why not let her body smash through the windshield?"

"Because she was on the passenger side of the car. It needed to look like she was driving. And I did it," Sharon said smugly. "Granted, it was a bit hard to drag her around to the driver's side, but I made it look like she'd tried to get out of the car after she'd crashed. And you believed it!" she crowed.

"One tiny detail you overlooked," Galloway said, deadpan. "The bruising from the seatbelt. It proved Molly was in the passenger seat and not behind the wheel."

Sharon's mouth dropped open when she realized her mistake.

"Then what happened? You walked back to the pub to retrieve your car? That's a heck of a walk," Galloway continued his interrogation.

"I waited until she died. Didn't take long. I couldn't risk someone coming along and saving her. Then, yes, I walked back to the pub. It took me almost three hours."

Galloway nodded at Sergeant Young, who stepped forward, whipped Sharon's hands behind her back, and cuffed her. "Sharon Mooney, you are under arrest for the murder of Molly Lewis and the suspected murder of multiple residents of the Firefly Bay Residential Aged Care Facility."

"You can't arrest me!" Sharon cried. "I'm needed here. They need me. My work isn't done."

"Oh, yes, it is." Sergeant Young pushed her toward the front doors, continuing to read her her rights as they went.

"Wow!" I breathed, watching as Young and Collier secured Sharon in the back of the police car. "She is delusional."

"That's what makes her dangerous," Galloway said, looping an arm around my shoulders. "She truly believes that she was helping by overdosing them on morphine. And in a place like this, who's going to bother with an autopsy?"

"It's just awful. And so sad."

"You're not wrong." Galloway sighed, then checked the time. "We'd better get moving, don't want to be late."

"For?"

"Your dad's birthday?"

"You're not going to the station?" I asked, and he shook his head.

"Sharon's not going anywhere. She can cool her heels in a cell tonight."

"If it wasn't Dad's birthday, I'd call it off," I admitted, following Galloway out to the parking lot where he was headed toward my car. I'd volunteered to drive because I'd thought he'd be going to the station with Sharon, and this way, I'd have my own car to get home. Seems that wasn't necessary after all.

"What? Why?" Galloway asked, waiting for me to unlock the car before climbing into the passenger seat.

I followed suit, sliding in behind the wheel. I smothered a yawn. "Because I'm tired. It's been a really full-on day."

"Oh." He looked crestfallen. "I enjoy dinner with your parents."

"Me too. Don't panic. We're still going, but let's not make it a late one. I need my beauty sleep."

"You are beautiful just as you are." He reached across and laid a hand on my thigh, and I rested my hand on top of it. Then two things happened simultaneously that nearly had me driving us off the road. First, the radio came on all by itself, blasting out *Black Magic* by Little Mix, then Molly appeared in the back seat.

"Holy heck!" I squeaked, over-correcting with a screech of tires. I may have peed myself a little.

Galloway latched onto the dash with both hands. "What was that about?" he gasped.

"Sorry. I think Molly just joined us. It is you, right?" I directed my words to the woman who'd appeared in the back seat with a bright floral top and brown curly hair. Leaning forward, I turned off the radio.

"Finally!" Molly said. "I've been following you around for ages, but you couldn't see or hear me."

Now I knew what it meant. All those times I'd heard that song? That was when Molly was near.

"Weird. Now is usually the time when the victim crosses over. Cos, you know, we solved your murder," I said.

"Who would've thought Sharon had it in her?" Molly leaned an arm around the back of my seat, wedging her body between the front seats. If you could call a ghost hovering in your vehicle wedging.

"Did you suspect her? Of prematurely helping the residents along to the ever after?" I asked.

"Not her. I thought it was Dean. He's a slimy piece of work. I tried to warn Angela about him. I knew he was up to no good, then when I discovered the missing morphine, it wasn't hard to put two and two together."

"But what I don't understand, aside from the missing drugs part, is how you knew the residents hadn't died naturally. How did you know it was a morphine overdose?"

"Because those residents weren't ill. They were old, yes, but they weren't near the end of life. Not in my opinion. So, I started to investigate. Quietly, mind you, that sort of thing is a touchy subject, and I didn't want to start a fuss if I was wrong."

"But you don't have access to the drug cabinet. How did you get around that without anyone knowing what you were up to?"

"Volunteered to do a spot audit." She shrugged. "No one likes doing it, so I put my hand up."

"And you were left alone? With the unlocked drug cabinet?"

"Appalling, isn't it?" Molly nodded. "Yep. One of the RNs unlocked it for me and left me to it."

"Obviously, it wasn't Sharon or Dean." I turned into my driveway, hitting the button to open the garage door. "But what about what you told Nick, that you were using your fake relationship with him as a cover, that you were seeing someone?"

"Pft, that was for Nick's benefit. He's such a sweetheart, he was really concerned that I was pretending to be his girlfriend with nothing in it for me, so to make him feel better, I told a little white lie that he'd be doing me a favor too."

Galloway tapped the clock on the dash. "You've got five minutes to freshen up, then we've got to leave."

"Why are you in a dead set hurry to get to Dad's?" I grumbled, sliding out from behind the wheel and slamming my door.

"I'm not," he protested. "I assume it's Molly you're talking to?"

"Yep." I filled him in on what we'd discussed while leading the way into the house, Molly trailing behind us.

"Molly!" The twelve ghosts who'd only recently stopped following me around and were content to wait in my living room lit up at the sight of the nurse.

"Hey, guys." Molly beamed, crossing to them, touching the arm of each ghost with a gentle hand, looking directly into their eyes and smiling. "Hi, Norma. Hi, Beverley. Hi, William. Hi, John. Hi, Elsie. Hi, Margaret. Hi, Ted. Hi, Edna. Hi, Erik. Hi, Ronald. Hi, Cecilia. Hi, Elizabeth." She did the rounds, giving them her undivided attention.

"I missed you," the one named Erik said and hugged her.

I almost cried. All this time, they'd been stuck, only able to say the word Angel, and now here they were, speaking and hugging the nurse who'd cared for them.

"I'm sorry I couldn't save you." Molly rubbed her hand up and down Erik's back.

"Your actions saved countless others," Cecilia stated. "I'm only sorry you ended up here with us."

There was the chatter of agreement, then Cecilia asked, "What happens now?"

"Now it's time to cross over." Molly beamed, and behind her, a white light glowed. "Come on, now, don't be scared. I'm coming right along with you; we'll all be together. Single file, please ladies and gents, step on through." She herded them through the light, one at a time, then turned, and with a final wave, said, "Tell Mom I love her." She stepped into the light, and my living room was devoid of ghosts. Except for Ben.

"Have they gone?" Galloway asked, approaching from behind to wrap his arms around me in a hug.

I nodded, a little choked up. I was happy and sad at the same time, but we'd gotten justice for Molly and the others, and that's what mattered.

"Right." I cleared my throat. "Five minutes you said?"

"You're down to three. Get a wriggle on." He grinned and tapped my butt.

* * *

"What happened to your face?" My brother Dustin gawked at my injuries.

"What happened to *your* face?" I shot back, ignoring him. There hadn't been enough time to put on a full face of makeup, but who was I kidding? All the makeup in the world wasn't going to hide the graze on my chin. I'd settled on a splash of water and a swipe of tinted moisturizer. A quick dab of mascara and some lip gloss had been the extent of my glamorization. Clean jeans and T-shirt, puke-free shoes, and I was good to go.

I'd wrapped Dad's whisky in a box, within a box, within a box, until it was the size of a microwave. Galloway gallantly carried it inside.

"Hello darling." Mom wrapped me in a hug, then pulled back, gently cupped my face, and sighed.

"It's okay, Mom," I assured her. "Nothing unusual."

"I know, dear, I know." She gently squeezed my cheeks before releasing me.

"Happy Birthday, Dad!" I beamed, wrapping my arms around Dad's waist and squeezing.

"Thanks, Doodlebug." He squeezed back. "What did you get me? Jock itch cream?"

"I heard you were running low." I nodded solemnly.

He rubbed his hands together with anticipation. "Excellent."

Galloway handed over the overwrapped parcel, and everyone gathered around while he dutifully unwrapped it. Not that it was a surprise. We went through the whole charade every single year. I'd buy single malt whisky and wrap it in a dozen boxes, and Dad would pretend he didn't know what it was.

Once the gift-giving was finished, Galloway made a beeline for baby Grace, scooping her out of Laura's arms to coo and pull faces at her. Grace waved her arms and giggled.

"Audrey, how are you? No, really, how are you?" Amanda sidled up next to me in her designer jeans and silk blouse, not a hair out of place. Despite having two kids who would run anyone ragged, Amanda was always immaculate, with no stains or tears, hair and makeup perfect. I felt like a positive frump in comparison.

I smiled at my sister-in-law. "I'm fine, Amanda. You? How's work?"

She ignored my question. "How did you do that?" She pointed to my chin.

"Tripped up the stairs."

"You know—" she began, only Dustin, her husband, warned, "Amanda."

"But she," Amanda whispered to him.

"Amanda," he warned again, one eyebrow arching. "We talked about this, remember?"

"You do know I'm standing right here and can hear you, right?" I said loudly.

Amanda had the grace to blush. "You're right. I'm sorry, that was rude."

"Lucky I'm the forgiving sort." I patted her back. "Why don't you go help Mom serve?" I suggested. "I'd do it, but you know me, I'd probably drop it all over the floor."

Amanda flashed a smile and did as I suggested, heading into the kitchen to help Mom. Not that Mom needed help. All she had to do was plate up the take-out delivery from Delgorno's. I just needed breathing space.

"She means well," Dustin said apologetically.

"I know she does." I smiled.

Brad, Laura's husband, approached with a glass of wine and pressed it into my hand. "You look like you could use this."

"You, as always, are a lifesaver."

"Okay, everyone!" Mom clapped her hands to get our attention. "Take a seat. Dinner is ready."

Dinner was a normal chaotic family affair. Madeline, fast approaching four, was too big for a highchair and now had her own seat at the table, much to her delight. Her little brother Nathaniel was thankfully confined to his highchair with a selection of food smooshed into the tray and down the front of his shirt. At the same age, his cousin, Isabelle, was in a highchair next to him, and baby Grace was asleep in her stroller. Amongst the noise, the food, and the wine, I felt at peace. This was family. This was home.

After dinner came the cake. It was ablaze with candles, and I'm amazed the smoke detector didn't go off. Of course, the cake was more for the kids' benefit than Dad's, but we all reaped the benefits. Galloway, who was sitting to my left, pushed back his chair and leaned toward the floor.

"What's up?" I asked. "Drop something?"

"Audrey," he said solemnly. I was busy shoveling cake into my mouth, so I didn't look at him until I heard startled gasps from around the table.

"Mmmm?" I finally said, turning to face him. "Oh, my God!" I squeaked, almost choking on the cake.

He was down on one knee. I glanced around the table, from my mom, whose eyes were full of tears, to Laura, who had the biggest smile I'd ever seen, to Amanda, who had her hands clasped to her heart and an awwww expression on her face. The menfolk just had blank looks, like they hadn't worked out what was happening yet. Because, of course, they couldn't see the ring box in Galloway's hand, just below the table line.

Galloway cleared his throat and started again. "Audrey."

I held up my hand to stop him, and Dustin groaned.

"No, wait," I said around my mouthful of cake. "I need to finish this, or I'm going to choke." So, the whole table watched me chew and chew and chew. It's really hard to swallow cake when your mouth has gone dry. I finally washed down the last crumbs with a gulp of wine, then turned back to Galloway. "Continue." My voice may have shaken just a tad.

He smiled and took my hand. "From the very first moment we met, when I saved you from being hit by a bus and you thanked me by hitting me in the nuts, I knew you were going to have a BIG impact on my life."

I grinned at the memory. He had saved me by grabbing me by the elbow and jerking me out of the path of the bus, only my momentum had swung me around, and I'd accidentally clocked him in the gonads. How sweet of him to remember.

"And boy, did you deliver," Galloway continued. "All the times we were chasing killers and catching thieves, you stole my heart. I can't wait to have more moments like these for the rest of our lives. Audrey Fitzgerald, will you marry me?"

"Even though I'm clumsy, and that probably won't be the last time I hit you in the nuts?" I whispered, blinking rapidly because the sight of him on one knee, holding a ring, was making me mist up.

"Even though," he whispered. "And, you know, just in case you're having a hard time making up your mind, despite the fact that your whole family agrees I'm a great catch," he continued, and everyone around the table snickered, "I promise to love every little bump, bruise, and graze."

That did it. Not that I'd needed extra convincing. "Yes!" I launched myself into his arms, tumbling us both to the floor in a tangle of limbs and laughter.

The ring box flew from his hand and rolled away under the table, and he lay there, with me sprawled on his chest, and laughed. "I can't believe you just did that."

"What? Said yes?" I frowned.

"No, that you knocked the ring out of my hand! I thought for sure you'd go for the diamond."

"That's what I would have done!" Laura piped up.

"I'll get it, Uncle Kwade," Madeline declared, sliding off her chair and crawling under the table. She scooped the box up in her little chubby hand and crawled across to us. "Here y'go," she said, then sat on her butt and watched with great interest while Galloway flicked open the box and pulled out the ring. I eased up so I was straddling his hips and held out my trembling left hand. Galloway slid the ring onto my ring finger, and I simply stared at it. It was stunning and simple and oh so me. A single solitaire.

Leaning down, I cupped his face and kissed him. "I love you."

"Love you too."

The noise level was deafening as my entire family whooped and hollered. Mom rushed to the kitchen to get the champagne she happened to have on ice; Amanda brought out the champagne glasses.

"Did they know?" I quirked a brow. And that's when I realized I'd finally done it. Not only nailed the hottest bachelor in town but raised one eyebrow independently of the other. A day worthy of celebration indeed.

* * *

Have you read the Ghost Detective shorts? This collection includes the novellas *Deck the Halls* and *What Ghost Around*. Read along as Audrey and the gang get in the Christmas spirit for the holidays, Ben receives an unexpected gift, and Santa turns up face-down in a pile of snow. Add in a tropical vacation, a surfing lesson gone awry, and the biggest litter box Thor has ever seen, and you've got two fun-filled murder mysteries. Ready to go sleuthing? www.JaneHinchey.com/GhostDetectiveShorts

AFTERWORD

Thank you for reading, if you enjoyed **Who Ghost There?,** please consider leaving a review. You can find a complete list of my books on my website at:

www.JaneHinchey.com

Also, if you'd like to sign up to receive emails with the latest news, exclusive offers, and more, you can do that here:

www.JaneHinchey.com/subscribe

And finally, I'd love to invite you to join my **VIP Readers group** where you get exclusive access to me, the opportunity to win one of the monthly signed paperback giveaways, join in live videos, get sneak peeks at works in progress and so much more. You can join us here:

www.JaneHinchey.com/LittleDevils

Thank you so much for taking a chance and reading my book - I do this for you.

xoxo

Jane

Read more by Jane

Find them all at
www.JaneHinchey.com/books

The Ghost Detective Mysteries

#1 Ghost Mortem

#2 Give up the Ghost

#3 The Ghost is Clear

#4 A Ghost of a Chance

#5 Here Ghost Nothing

#6 Who Ghost There?

#7 Wild Ghost Chase

Witch Way Paranormal Cozy Mystery Series

#1 Witch Way to Magic & Mayhem

#2 Witch Way to Romance & Ruin

#3 Witch Way Down Under

#4 Witch Way to Beauty & the Beach

#5 Witch Way to Death & Destruction

#6 Witch Way to Secrets & Sorcery

The Midnight Chronicles

#1 One Minute to Midnight

#2 Two Minutes Past Midnight

#3 Third Strike of Midnight

PARANORMAL ROMANCE/URBAN FANTASY

The Awakening Series

#1 First Blade

#2 First Witch

#3 First Blood

About Jane

Jane Hinchey is an Aussie author who loves to write cozy mysteries with plenty of laughs and mayhem along the way - who says murder can't be fun? Her bestselling Ghost Detective series combines all of this into an intriguing melting pot of paranormal danger, fast-paced action, and plenty of tongue-in-cheek snarky humor.

Jane lives in the mortal realm with her non-paranormal man, two cats whose paranormal status is yet to be determined (she did catch them trying to open a portal in the kitchen that one time), a turtle named Squirt (who is massive!).

Sometimes, when the supernatural chaos calls for a different kind of story, she writes under the name Zahra Stone, where the characters you meet are as sexy as they are deadly.

Learn more or sign up for her newsletter at
www.JaneHinchey.com